BEYOND THE GAME

CHICAGO RED TAILS
BOOK 3

SUSAN RENEE

Beyond THE GAME

To Jenn, Jennifer, Kristan and Stephani.
Thank you for pushing me WAY outside my comfort zone
and always having faith in me.
Even on those days when I don't have any in myself.

"I think I'm in a someone-needs-to-fuck-me-out-of-this-mood kind of mood."

Hawken nearly spits out his beer. "Don't look at me, man. You know I love you, Dex, but I don't love you enough for that."

I turn to him, dismayed. "You mean to tell me you wouldn't fuck me if my life literally depended on it?"

His brows raise. "Does it?"

"No."

"Then no. I might consider it if, and only if, we were literally the last two human beings on this earth, but other than that, my dick paddles for the pretty pink canoe."

"Thanks, I guess." I roll my eyes.

"Why the hell are you in a mood, man? We're in fucking Key West. We've just spent the day at the beach and finished a wedding rehearsal. Our teammate is marrying the love of his life and we're sitting here enjoying paradise while drinking. What could be better than that?"

"Pussy," I state. "Petting pussy. Eating pussy. Fucking

pussy. I'm good at two things in this world. Hockey and sex. And right now, I don't have either of those two things."

"Aww, are you fuckstrated, big brother?" Rory steps up to the bar, overhearing Hawk and I talking. I almost laugh at her made-up word, but I don't because she's right.

"Hell, yes. I'm fuckstrated. I came here for the sun, the sand, and the sex."

"Okay, so what's the problem?" Hawk asks, taking another sip of his beer.

"Nobody knows who I am down here."

Rory frowns. "And that's bad because...?"

"After games, the bunnies come out to play. They just want to fuck a hockey player to say they fucked a hockey player so it's easy picking. But not one person has recognized me since we arrived in Florida. It's a little annoying."

Rory laughs. "You pitiful thing. I'm sure you'll find some willing piece of ass eventually. You might just have to work for it this time." I give her an annoyed stare and her eyes grow huge, a smile widening across her face. "I know. The nerve of these Florida women, right?"

"Ugh. You're so annoying. Why did you come down here again?"

She smirks. "To help plan the best beach wedding I have ever seen. You must admit, the rehearsal was outstanding. And tomorrow Charlee will look like a fucking goddess."

I sip my beer and nod in agreement. "I have no doubt."

It will be a beautiful wedding and really, I couldn't be happier for Milo and Charlee.

Rory pinches my cheek the way our grandmother

would after not seeing us for long stretches of time. "And yes, Dexter. You'll make the cutest flower girl ever."

"Damn right he will." Hawk laughs, clinking his beer bottle with mine. "I bet those petals aren't easy to toss on a windy beach."

"You can say that again. I'll have to stretch for the job and everything."

"Well, if anyone deserves to get laid tonight, it's you, big brother. Do you need some help? I could pick out a couple hot ladies for you. There are a few sitting by the pool right now."

"Get outta here." I shove her teasingly, but Hawk catches her before she falls backwards. "I don't need a wing-sister. I can catch tail all by myself."

"Good." She straightens up. "Hawk, I need a partner for pool. Will you help me kick Colby and Carissa's asses?"

"What?" I perk up. "Why wouldn't you ask me? I'm your fucking brother. We're blood."

"Because you're way too fuckstrated. Duh." She rolls her eyes. "Go get laid. You'll feel better." She gestures toward a small group of women dancing by the pool. "Seriously, if I were you, I would opt for one of those." She pats my shoulder with excitement spread across her face. "Oooh and you should totally use your old pick-up line from high school. You know that transformer one!"

"Shut up, Rory. We don't talk about the transformer pick-up line anymore."

"Oooh," Hawken laughs. "This is one I haven't heard! What's the transformer pick-up line?"

She waves him off. "Something about being Optimus Fine."

She laughs and Hawken cackles as I rub my forehead, my annoyance for my sister growing by the second.

"Oh, fuck, please use that one, Dex. Let me know how it goes."

"Come on," Rory says to Hawk as she steals him away. "We have a game of pool to win. Catch you later, Sexy Dexy." She winks and laughs as the two of them walk away.

"Do NOT call me Sexy Dexy!"

She cackles even louder as they round the patio to the bar. Shaking my head in laughter, I finish off my beer and am about to order another when a woman steps up to the bar next to me. She orders a sex on the beach and a Long Island iced tea and then turns to me.

"Hey."

"Hi." I give her my best smolder, but she giggles in response.

"Yeah, that won't work too well on me big guy. I like to lick pussy too." Her smile and wink make me laugh out loud.

"Fuck, nobody has ever said that to me before."

"I mean, don't get me wrong. It's a sexy smolder for sure. And it would work on my friend over there if you're interested." She gestures to a woman lounging by the pool in a black bikini, her golden hair piled creatively on top of her head. I can't make out her exact features from here but at first glance, she doesn't appear to be a troll.

I cock my head. "Are you trying to set me up with your friend?"

She shrugs. "Depends."

Well, this is interesting.

"On?"

"Are you a nice guy?"

"Uh, I'm literally the nicest guy. Like, ever."

She smirks. "Why don't I believe you?"

"Ugh, okay. In all honesty, my buddy, Milo, is the nicest guy ever, but he's gettin' hitched tomorrow so he's off the market. If you'll allow me to be nice guy by proxy..."

That makes her laugh. "Alright, so you're a nice guy. We'll go with that. Is nice guy single?"

"Fuck yeah. Nice guy doesn't commit. He's nice to everyone."

"You good in bed? Or are you just, you know, average?"

I laugh at her question. "Uh, I'm more than good. Trust me."

"You know that's what they all say, right?"

"And you know there isn't a guy on this earth who is willing to admit he's just average, right?"

"Fair point." She laughs again and raises her glass to clink with my empty beer bottle. "Look, I invited my friend to Florida with me to celebrate her divorce from a nasty ass piece of cheating shit."

Narrowing my eyes, I stare down the woman who is now double fisting the drinks she ordered. "So, you want me to pity fuck her? Is that what you're asking me?"

"Uh, no." She scoffs. "She doesn't need nor want anyone's pity. She's happy to be moving onward and upward. I'm merely suggesting you hit on her. Make her feel sexy. Maybe boost her confidence a little before she starts her life over again. It's always nice to go on vacation and feel noticed, right?"

She's not wrong.

Wasn't I just saying something like that?

"And hey, if things work out and you both get to experience a little non-committal play time, what's the harm in that?"

She slides the sex on the beach over to me. "This is hers. I'm going back to our room to shower and pack. It was nice meeting you, nice guy who is supposedly good in bed."

"Yeah." I nod, watching her walk away from the pool area and back toward the elevators. "Nice to meet you too..."

My eyes shift to where the woman's friend was sitting by the pool, but she's not there now. I spy a girl in a black bikini headed toward the very bar I'm sitting at and holy fucking shit, I am one lucky son of a bitch.

Tendrils of her hair fly around her face in the wind off the beach. Her skin kissed by several days in the sun. She's not one of those stick-thin barbie doll types. On the contrary, this woman has curves in all the right places for a man like me, and she walks with confidence, which I love to see.

I'm merely suggesting you hit on her. Make her feel sexy.

Maybe boost her confidence a little before she starts her life over again.

Seems easy enough.

I guess it's now or never.

Just as she makes it to the bar, I meet her and blurt out, "If you were a transformer, you would be Optimus Fine."

What.

The.

Fuck.

Did.

I.

6

Just.

Do.

Oh my God!

Did I seriously just throw her the Transformers pick up line?

Fucking Rory!

My feet planted firmly in place, my body goes rigid and I swear my dick just shriveled up and died of disappointment. This is the end of my life. Tomorrow's headline will read *Twenty-nine-year-old man dies of dick disappointment when using Transformers pick-up line on hot chick.*

Fuck me.

Blondie laughs as my cheeks redden. She places her hand on her hip and tilts her head. "So, what if I prefer Bumblebee?"

I shake my head, still horribly embarrassed. "I am so sorry. I want to say I don't know where that even came from except it's totally my sister's fault and I swear I'm usually a whole lot smoother than this. I'm slightly mortified right now."

She laughs again and my chest lightens. "Don't be. You got my attention, didn't you?"

"Uh, yeah." I chuckle to myself. "I guess I did." I slide her drink toward her. "Look, I don't ever recommend taking a drink from a strange guy, but your friend just ordered this for you and then said she was heading to her room to shower and pack. She asked me to give this to you. I promise I'm a nice guy."

"You're safe ma'am," the bartender adds. "I made the drink and I've been right here the whole time."

She reads the guy's nametag. "Thank you, Barry."

"You're welcome, ma'am."

"See? Told you. I'm a nice guy." I gesture to Barry the bartender for another beer and notice the pretty woman's eyes floating up my body, taking note of the tattoos on my chest and shoulder. I don't miss the few seconds her gaze lingers on my lower abs either.

Yep. Check me out baby.

"So, my roommate left me, huh?"

"Looks that way, yeah. She said you wanted to soak up the last of the sun before you leave tomorrow."

"She's right. I wanted to watch the sunset."

"They're definitely beautiful here. What's your name?

"Uh..." Her eyes narrow as she glances at me. All of me. "My name is Amanda."

I cock my head. "Is that your real name, Amanda?"

She nods. "Sure. Amanda Hugginkis. That's me."

Cute. So, we're doing the fake name thing? Alright, I'll play.

I huff out a laugh. "Well Amanda Hugginkis, it's nice to meet you. I'm uh...Ben. Ben Dover."

She grins back at me. "Nice to meet you, Ben. Care to join me in a sunset viewing?"

I clink my bottle with her glass. "Sure."

I follow her out to the beachside patio where she steps into one of the several open hot tubs. I step in behind her and take her hand so she doesn't slip. She sits along the edge where we can see the ocean and admire the colorful canvas the sun is creating for us right in front of our eyes, and I maneuver myself next to her.

"So, where are you from?" I ask, trying to make small talk.

"Michigan."

"That's quite a distance from Key West."

She nods. "Damn right it is."

"Uh oh." I chuckle. "Something about that response doesn't sound good."

"Nope, it's all good now." She shakes her head.

"Oh, okay. Good. Are you here for a reason?" I already know the answer but she doesn't know I know.

She returns my question. "Are you?"

"Uh, yeah. I am. My buddy's getting married tomorrow. We're down here on a group vacation."

"Ah. Well, you might want to avoid me then."

As if.

"Why do you say that?"

"Because I'm here celebrating my divorce."

"Celebrating, huh? So, this is a divorce you're happy about?"

She nods emphatically. "Fuck, yeah. Now. He's nothing but a lying, cheating, piece of shit."

"Cheater? Ugh what a fucking twat monster. I'm sorry that happened to you."

"No, twat Monster would be my best friend who was fucking him in our bed when I walked in on them."

"Oh shit!"

"Yeah."

"Wow. What did you do?"

"What could I do? He tried to tell me it didn't mean anything, which pissed her off, and she tried to apologize out the ass but it was too late. I told them both to burn in Hell."

9

I raise my hand next to her, signaling my high-five. "Fuck yeah, you did! Good for you, Amanda."

She slaps my hand with a smile. "Is it bad that I don't feel the least bit of remorse for the way I left things with him?"

"I can't even say that depends because no fucking way should you feel bad. But just for shits and giggles, how did you leave things? I mean other than telling them to burn in Hell?"

A proud grin plays on her face. "When he went to work the next day, I threw every one of his belongings outside on his front lawn, flushed the house keys, and moved out."

"Oh shit. That's savage. Way to go tiger!" I shake my head. "Nothing wrong with that at all. Cheers to doing what you needed to do."

"Thank you. It happened months ago. The divorce only just became official, thank God. It's good to finally feel free."

"I can imagine."

"Ever been married, Ben?" she asks.

"Hell no."

Her brows raise. "Oooh. Touchy subject, huh?"

"Nah." I shrug. "Just not sure I'm marriage material."

"Meaning you don't want to commit."

I tip my beer to my lips. "Somethin' like that." Wanting to get the subject off me, I throw more questions her way.

"What do you do?"

"I'm an elementary school teacher. I actually just interviewed for a new position teaching first grade in a new town."

"So new freedom, new job, new life, huh?"

She swallows a sip of her drink. "That's the plan."

"And this trip is for celebrating all that?"

She tips her drink back and swallows. "Yep."

"Good for you. Have you done anything fun since you got here?"

"Yeah, of course. We snorkeled, we shopped, we spent time on the beach. I read a couple books, we danced our hearts out at a few clubs and now here I am, watching the sunset on my last night here."

"Excellent," I tell her. "Sounds like you knew exactly what you needed and went for it."

She looks out at the ocean. "Yeah, I guess."

Her demeanor changes slightly. She doesn't make eye contact, but continues to sip her drink, staring out at the water.

"If you've had such a momentous week, why don't you look happy? Is it because you're heading home tomorrow?"

"That's part of it, sure."

"What's the other part? Can I ask?"

Her cheeks redden and she shakes her head. I think she's embarrassed. "It's stupid. You'll just laugh at me...or think I'm weird."

I lift a few fingers. "Scouts honor. I won't laugh."

"Were you actually a boy scout?"

"Nope," I chuckle. "But I promise I won't laugh. Consider me a stranger you can tell anything to. Because after tonight you won't see me ever again so what does it matter?"

"True."

"See? I'm all ears. Tell me your regrets." I lean back against the hot tub, my arms outstretched, enjoying the view of both the setting sun on the beach and the pretty woman sitting here with me.

She gazes out at the ocean one more time and then we tip our glasses drinking back quite a bit. My brows rise as I watch her drink down the colorful liquid. Her swallow is impressive and suddenly I'm imagining her swallowing something else.

"I regret coming here and not hooking up with someone."

Is this some sort of joke?

Did Rory put her up to this?

"Ahh, so is this your pick-up schtick?"

"What?"

"You know." I wink. "Tell the sexy new guy you're starting life over and regret not hooking up with someone to really...you know, celebrate? Amanda Hugginkis needs a man to hug and kiss?"

She turns and looks me straight in the eye, a serious expression on her face, and mutters, "Who said you were sexy?"

"Oooh! Ouch!" I throw my hand over my heart. "You wound me!"

She's laughing though so if this really is some sort of pick-up experience, she got me good.

"I'm sorry," she giggles. "But you kind of walked right into that one, but also, oh, my God! I swear this isn't that." She lays a hand over her face, mildly embarrassed. "God I probably do sound like a desperate little fuck, don't I? Ugh I'm so sorry. I didn't mean it like that at all. I just..." She shakes her head. "I don't know. I had this fantasy that I would come to the Keys and meet someone who would like...rearrange my guts if you know what I mean."

"Do they sell those somewhere around here? Gut rearrangers?"

She laughs. "You know what I mean."

"I know exactly what you mean." I try to control my reaction because fuck yes, I know what she means.

She lifts her face to the sky as she breathes in the sea air. "I was hoping for this..." She rests a hand on her chest, drawing my eye to her two beautiful breasts clad in small pieces of black material. A man could most definitely get lost between those babies. "Soul destroying orgasm like I've never experienced before. A reward for leaving my lying, cheating husband, you know? A night of epic sex and ever-lasting memories that he could never provide to take home with me. Something positive to think about instead of how Mr. Douche ruined my life."

Holy fuck.

Did her lesbian friend really exist back there at the bar or was she some sort of guardian angel?

Suddenly my mouth is dry and I'm finding it hard to swallow.

"He didn't ruin your life."

"No?"

I shake my head. "If things wouldn't have happened the way they did, you wouldn't be sitting here with me right now. In fact, what's his address? I think I need to send him a thank you note."

She laughs heartily. "For what?"

Fuck this.

Whatever this is.

13

Whatever her intentions are or were.

I'm going for it.

"For giving me the opportunity to show the woman who once loved him what an epic mistake he made. For giving me the opportunity to show the woman he once loved what a night of passionate sex is supposed to feel like. How much her beautiful body deserves to be pleasured." I lean in a little closer and murmur to her, "What it feels like to orgasm so much and so hard that she forgets her damn name."

The small gasp and heavy sigh that comes from her mouth in response has my dick so hard I could bend her over this hot tub and rearrange her guts right the fuck now.

"You might not know this about me, Amanda, but rear-ranging guts is sort of my specialty."

Her face reddens and she shakes her head. "You don't have to do that."

"Do what?"

"Pretend you're coming on to me. It's sweet of you though." As the sun has finally set, she stands, turning toward the beach and picking up her glass. "I should prob-ably go. I need to pack."

What?

No!

She can't go!

I stand quietly behind her and thank the Gods it's dusk enough to not be noticed by copious amounts of people. "Amanda?"

"Yeah?"

I wrap a hand around her waist and pull her against my

chest, my hand resting on the warmed skin of her abdomen. "Who said anything about pretending?"

"Ben..." She breathes.

"I happen to think you're a goddamn knockout, and I would be honored to make every single one of your fantasies come true before this night is over."

She turns her head enough to try to see my face behind her. "What are you saying exactly?"

"I'm saying, you want a night of epic sex. Soul destroying orgasms and memories you won't soon forget. I can give that to you."

"Why should I trust you?"

"You shouldn't." I kiss the side of her neck. "But I promise you I'm not a creep. I'm just a guy who knows how to treat a woman in bed. If I wanted to pull one over on you, I would've done it already with your drink, remember?"

She contemplates my reasoning for a moment and then turns her head back to the ocean. "Anything I want?"

"You name it, Sweetheart."

"I don't want gentle."

I tug her against me a little harder. "Good. I'm anything but."

"I want you to press me up against the wall and..."

"And what, Amanda?" I murmur into her ear. "Finger you until you can't stand anymore? Get on my knees and lick your sweet pussy until you're shaking? Or simply lower you onto my dick and drive into you until you're literally screaming."

"Oh, my God. All of it. That sounds...wonderful."

I reach for her other hand and bring it behind her,

placing it over my hardened cock. She palms me, her gasp
not taking me by surprise. It's not the first time a woman
has reacted this way.

"Holy shit, you're pierced?"

She turns and looks down at my crotch currently
covered by my swim trunks. I merely smirk and smooth my
thumb over her cheek. "Only one way to find out. Tell me
you want this and I'll make it a night you won't soon
forget."

"I'm all yours."

"You're not mine, Sweetheart. But I'll absolutely ruin
you for any man who comes after me." I offer her my hand.
"Let's go."

2

TATUM AKA AMANDA

Ben leads me to his resort room, which is lavishly luxurious compared to mine. It's more of a suite with a massive bed, a seating area with an over-sized couch and television, a kitchen and dining area, and a private balcony with every comfort imaginable looking over the beach below. As it's dark now, I can only assume the view in the morning is incredible.

Just who is this Ben Dover and how does he afford such an upscale room?

As I peer over the balcony, Ben steps up behind me, wrapping his arms around my waist and kissing the side of my neck just behind my ear.

"This is your only chance to change your mind. If you want to walk, I won't stop you." He brings both hands up to my breasts and grabs them with force, pinching my nipples and twisting with just enough pressure to cause a spark of lust to shoot through me from my chest to my feet. "But if you stay, orgasm number one is happening right here, right fucking now."

I lose all my breath in a half whimper, half moan and allow my head to fall back on Ben's shoulder. Good God should I be feeling this good right now? We've barely even started.

"I don't want to go anywhere," I breathe. "Not until you've given me what you promised."

"One night," he growls, licking my ear. "As many orgasms as you can physically handle and then one more to help you remember me." He slips a hand into my bikini bottoms, his fingers reaching between my legs. "Fucking hell, you're drenched for me already."

Holy hell, his fingers feel amazing sliding through me.

Spreading me.

Rubbing me.

"This is more excitement than my pussy has seen in well over a year. You'll have to forgive her eagerness."

"Babe, there is nothing to forgive. It'll be my absolute pleasure to give you an unforgettable night. And I'm going to start right here with this soft, wet pussy that feels so fucking good in my hand." The heel of his hand rests against my pussy, rubbing my clit as two long fingers push inside and swirl against my G-spot.

"Oh, my God, Ben." I gasp. "Holy shit!"

"You like that?"

"Mhmm."

"I can tell you do. You're soaking my fingers. You're going to come, and soon. I can feel it."

"Yes."

"Good girl."

Oh, my God, he just called me a good girl.

Why does that turn me on even more?

He kneads my breast with his other hand, pinching and rolling my nipple, and then moves to the other breast. All the while circling his fingers inside me, curling his fingers up. Though the breeze is warm against my skin on the balcony, it's not enough air to keep me from breaking out into a sweat. My legs shake with my first impending orgasm.

"Oh...God, I'm going to—"

"Come on my hand, Amanda. Let me feel this pretty pussy clench around my fingers, and when they do, I'm going to clean you out with my tongue."

He places his hand around my neck, forcing my face around so he can kiss me, and it's all I can do not to fall apart instantly. His tongue dives between my lips at the same time his fingers thrust into me. My body quivers, my knees get weak, and I start to fall as my climax rips through me.

"Ben! Oh...God!"

"That's it, Babe. Shit, you're so fucking beautiful like this. Coming in my arms. Squeezing my fingers. Soon Baby, this sweet pussy will clamp around my cock."

"My legs," I pant breathlessly. "My legs are shaking."

"I've got you, Babe. Just relax. Ride it out." He drags a hand under my legs and lifts me against him, cradling me against his body as he carries me to the oversized couch where he tosses me playfully. I let out a squeal and he's quickly on his knees, yanking my bikini bottoms off. The feral growl that comes out of him before his tongue dives between my legs is one of the sexiest sounds I've ever heard.

His tongue circles my clit softly several times in a row,

lapping at my arousal like a thirsty animal as I squirm and wriggle on the couch unable to control myself.

"So, fucking sweet. I could eat you for days and never tire."

I throw a hand across my face. "It's too much, Ben."

"Never, Baby. It's not too much. In fact, it's not enough." He helps to lift me, turning me onto my stomach and then lifts my hips in the air while my head rests on a couch pillow. "Much better. Fucking beautiful. He slips his tongue inside me and then drags it lazily all the way to my ass. The warm sensation of his tongue on my tight puckered hole causes me to heave forward, but Ben grabs my hips and pulls my body back against his face.

"Fuuuuuck yes! Right there. Oh, my God!"

He doesn't stop and I don't want him to. He nips at my ass cheek and then spanks me before diving between my legs for more. He sucks at my arousal, licking and circling his tongue.

Lick.

Suck.

Circle.

Lick.

Suck.

Circle.

He sits on the floor just below me, his head between my knees and then leans back and lowers my body over his face.

Oh, my God!

He tugs at my sensitive flesh with his teeth and all I can think about is I was today years old when I finally realized this is what a man eating me out is supposed to feel like.

And it is everything.

My breathing quickens and my body begins to tremble as my next orgasm builds and I'm helpless to stop it.

"Bennnnnn!"

"Fucking dripping for me, Babe. Goddamn, I can't wait to be inside you. Come on. Give it up for me." His tongue thrusts inside me along with a couple fingers curling along the inside, and I scream out.

"YES! Fuck! I'm coming!"

"Come on my tongue, Baby. I want to taste my reward." He continues to suck on my clit even as I convulse around him, only slowing when I start to go weak in my knees once again.

While I'm regaining my composure, I see Ben pull a condom from his suitcase and then pull his swim trunks off. He palms his stiff cock, running his hand up and down its length with a hiss.

Holy hell...

Look at him...

Prince Albert piercing.

Fuck, I bet that feels amazing.

It's...

It's so...

"Glorious."

A small smirk curves across his face. "I'm glad you like what you see, Baby."

He rips open his condom packet and sheaths himself and then lifts me from the couch. "Wrap your legs around me. You're about to get your next wish because I need to be inside you."

Before I can even remember what that next wish is, he's

slamming me up against the wall, his hands holding mine over my head and his mouth covering my nipple.

"You ready for my cock Amanda? Tell me you want my cock."

"God yes. Please, Ben."

"You have me so goddamn hard. I can't think straight. I need to fuck."

Breathless, my mouth opens and I gasp for air. "Then what are you waiting for?"

He bends his knees and swipes his cock through my arousal, coating himself, and then thrusts his hips up, pulling me down on his cock. "Fuuuuuck."

He stops for a minute, his forehead landing on mine.

"You okay?"

He closes his eyes and inhales a deep breath. "I had no idea you would be this incredibly tight."

"I'm sorr—"

"Don't you fucking apologize. This is the best fucking feeling in the world." He lets go of my hands above my head. "Wrap your arms around my neck because I'm about to fuck you hard. It's time to rearrange your guts."

"Oh, my God, yes, Ben. Yes please."

And just like that he becomes a feral savage beast of a lover, crashing into me over and over as hard as he can, grunting with every slam. I moan loud enough I'm sure several rooms down can hear me.

"Oh, fuck, yes!" I scream.

He continues his magnificent assault but steps back a foot so we're at a better angle. His head falls back as he thrusts again and again and again, his piercing hitting my G-spot every single time.

Best. Sex. Ever.

"Ah, shit," he says, railing me as he stares down at our connection. "It's so fucking good. I'm going to come, Baby."

"Me too. Oh, my God, it's never been this good before."

"Squeeze my cock, Baby. Come all over me. I want to feel you."

He pushes and pushes until my body lets go for a shocking third time.

Holy shit!

I've only ever had one orgasm at a time!

I scream out as my body seizes and I tighten my grip on Ben's neck.

He tightens his arms around me and drives into me a few more times as my orgasm washes over me. "Ahh fuck, yeah."

And then he stills.

His breathing is heavy and his growls are triumphant.

His body stops, but his cock pulses inside me. He nuzzles his face between my chest and my shoulder blade and I suddenly feel this overwhelming connection to him.

Which is silly as we barely know each other and will only be together for a short while longer. It's not like we'll ever see each other again, but maybe that's why I'm feeling this need to make an impression. So, he doesn't just remember me as another tight pussy he fucked on vacation.

I want to please him.

I want to pleasure him.

I want him to remember me.

He pulls out and rips off his condom, tossing it to the floor all while holding on to me, and then carries me to the bed, my legs and arms still wrapped around him. He lowers me to his huge bed and lies down next to me. His cock is still at the ready. Leaning over, he presses his lips to mine in a slower, lazy dance of our tongues.

Wanting to feel him, experience him, in all ways, I bravely wrap my hand around his cock and he hisses.

"Fuuuuck, Amanda."

"You're still impressively hard."

He smiles. "Because he knows he's not done."

"Oh, is that so?"

"Mhmm. There's still so much more of you to devour, Baby."

"I want to taste you."

He huffs out a soft chuckle. "Come and get it, Babe. If you want to suck me dry, have at it. I won't stop you."

He lies back down and wraps a hand around his cock, stroking himself as I watch. How on earth it is so damn sexy to watch a man stroke himself? I'll never know, but all I want to do right now is run my tongue over him.

Suck him.

Devour him.

I shimmy myself between his legs, his eyes trained on me as his hand pumps slowly up and down. I slide my hands up the inside of his thighs. He closes his eyes at my feather light touch but they're wide open when I slip my fingers around his balls, rolling them in my hand, tugging on them with stimulating pressure.

"Damn. Yeah, just like that, Baby. Feels so damn good."

His legs widen more as I cover his hand with my own over his shaft and he lets me take over. There's something about being given control of his body that emboldens me.

I want to rock his world.

I want to see him desperate for me.

I want to make this man come all on my own.

Wetting my lips, I grip his cock and lower my head over him, dragging my tongue slowly up his length until I reach his prince albert piercing, flicking my tongue over it lightly.

"Mother fuck." His hands gather my hair at the back of my head so he can watch what I do to him. I swirl my tongue over the tip and then take him deep into my mouth until he hits the back of my throat before pulling back.

"Fucking phenomenal, Amanda," he groans when I repeat the same movement, taking his entire cock into my mouth and pulling back up, sucking on his length. His hand still grasping my hair, he lightly pushes my head back down.

"Take it all for me, Baby. Swallow my cock."

I do as he requests only gagging a few times as I open wider for him and take his entire cock into my mouth, moaning against him as I pull back up.

"That's my good girl. Fucking divine."

I pop off his cock, licking down his shaft and around his balls, bringing each one into my mouth, rolling them between my lips.

Ben's eyes roll back in his head as his breathing quickens. "Fucking hell."

Knowing I have him in a vulnerable spot, I take things one step further and gently push his legs back toward his chest, his ass now bared for me.

"What are you—ooooh my...fucking Christ," he moans when I circle my tongue around his tightly puckered hole and then lick my way to his balls.

He's panting now, his eyes squeezed closed as he tries to control himself. "That is...fucking amazing."

"You like that?"

"Like it? Baby I think I'm going to explode even more than I did inside you and it's all because of your sweet little tongue. Please don't stop."

"As you wish."

I repeat my movements, circling his ass and trailing my tongue to his balls, stroking his cock and then doing the same thing all over again. Once I feel there's enough lubrication at the back, I lower my mouth over his cock, and slowly push my finger inside him.

"Holy shit!" He gasps. "Amanda! Fuck!"

I curl my finger inside, stroking his prostate as I suck him off, flicking his piercing on every up turn.

I suck faster.

Harder.

He groans louder.

"Baby, I'm going to come."

Moaning against his cock, I stroke my finger inside him with a little more pressure sliding in and out.

In and out.

Ben's breathing is sporadic as he starts to lose control and finally, he explodes, the tangy taste of his cum on my tongue as I swallow down every last drop.

It takes him a few minutes to come down from his unexpected high, but when he does, his demeanor is changed. He is no longer the sex-crazed savage lover he was when our time here began. Now he stares at me with shock and awe.

I think I rendered him speechless.

He slides a hand behind my head and pulls me to him, kissing me reverently and then leaning his forehead against mine.

"That was..." he breathes. "I..."

"Incredible?"

"That's putting it mildly." He nods against me. "But yes. What you did..."

He doesn't finish his statement because he can't think of the words.

"Ben, I haven't come with the help of a man in so long I almost forgot what it feels like. You helped rekindle that feeling for me. I just wanted to repay the favor."

"Fucking hell, you...I've never...Christ, I can't even form words."

Smiling, I kiss his cheek. "Good. I'll take that as a compliment." I kiss him again. "I'm just going to use the little girl's room to freshen up. I'll be right back."

"I'll definitely be right here. I don't think I could move if I tried."

Gazing at myself in the bathroom mirror, I take a deep breath and smile. Never in a million years did I expect a night like this to happen while on vacation. Hopeful for sex? Sure. But sex like what we just did? I didn't even know such an epic experience existed.

Once I finish my business and wash my hands, I pick up the small bottle of mouthwash on the sink and swish a little of it through my mouth and then comb my fingers through my just-fucked hair.

"That's better."

A little unsure of what he might want now that we've

done the deed, I swallow back any nerves I may have and open the door to rejoin my sexy one-night stand.

"Hey, if you feel like..." I stop in my tracks.

The sight of this man laying spread eagle on his bed, his eyes closed and sleeping peacefully brings an unexpected smile to my face.

I did that to him.

You go, Tatum!

I've still got it.

I can still pleasure a man into exhaustion.

And that's something I can be proud of.

Padding softly around the room, I slip my bikini back on, and then pull a sheet over Ben's bottom half, memorizing the impressive size of his cock and thanking the sex Gods for giving me this unforgettable experience. He doesn't budge when I cover him so I know this is my time to leave. We agreed to one night and several orgasms and we both got what we wanted. I can respect that. As much as I would love to curl up with that husky, hard body and fall asleep in his arms, only to wake up and do it all over again, I have a flight to catch in the morning. The last thing I want to do is come off as desperate, so I simply blow him a kiss, the man who will forever be my greatest *sexperience*, and then slip out into the hallway.

"Goodnight Ben Dover. And thank you."

3
DEX

KNOCK, KNOCK, KNOCK!

Y ou know those mornings when you open your eyes and you can't recall ever shutting them to begin with and don't know how or when you fell asleep but you've clearly been out cold for a long time?

Yeah. That's me.

Sunshine glows bright against my face, my sinfully sore and naked body already feeling the sticky humidity that comes with any Florida vacation.

Or maybe it's the fact I left my patio doors open last night.

Last night...

Amanda...

A satisfied smirk spreads across my face as I recall the details of last night.

My fingers inside her as she looked over the balcony.

The taste of her sweet pussy on my tongue.

Her voice as I made her come not once, not twice, but three times.

The feeling of her hands on me.

Her mouth on me.

Her...finger...inside me.

"Fuck, that was hot," I whisper to myself, my dick hardening at the thought.

Just then there's a beep and my door swings open.

"Dex Foster, you had better have a good reason f— OH MY GOD! What are you even doing?" Rory shouts as she covers her eyes with her hands. "MY EYES! MY EYES!"

I jump from the bed, shocked to see my sister in my room screaming at me while Hawken leans against the doorway smiling in amusement, his arms folded over his chest. My hands go straight to my junk trying to cover myself from my sister.

"What the fuck, Rory? Don't you fucking knock?"

"WE DID KNOCK, YOU PERV! SEVERAL TIMES! HOW COULD YOU NOT HEAR US? FOR THE LOVE OF CHRIST, PUT THAT THING AWAY!"

"I'm trying! You could give me a fucking minute!" I grab a pair of my boxer briefs from my suitcase and begin to pull them on.

"You don't have a minute, dumbass! You're going to be late to the wedding."

I freeze in place as my head snaps to Rory and Hawken. Both of them are dressed and ready for Milo and Charlee's big day.

"Fuck! What time is it?"

Rory huffs. "Would you kindly put your penis away so I don't have to throw up in my mouth?"

"Oh, for fuck's..." I pull up my briefs and then stare at my sister.

"It's eleven o'clock, Dex," Hawken finally answers my question with a smirk. "We're needed at the beach in thirty."

I push my hand through my hair, frustrated that I overslept. "Shit. I'll be there."

Rory stands against the wall with her arms crossed.

"What are you doing?"

"I'm waiting for you," she states. "I'm not letting you ruin this day for Milo and Charlee."

"I don't need help getting showered or dressed. Unless...I mean, unless you want to wash my balls for me? That might save me a minute."

She mimics throwing up and holding it in her mouth.

"I didn't think so. I'll shower and be right down."

She rolls her eyes. "Like I haven't heard that before."

"Oh, my God, Rory. I won't even take my morning shit, okay? Hawk, get her out of here, will you?"

"I don't know, this is sort of entertaining." He laughs but when he sees I'm not laughing, he takes Rory by the arm. "Come on Ror. You should go check on Charlee. She's more important anyway."

She points to me. "If you're not downstairs in ten minutes, I'm giving your flower girl job to Quinton."

"You wouldn't dare." I glare at her.

"Try me!" Finally, she storms out of my room, letting the door slam behind her.

I breathe in a deep breath and release it slowly, going

31

over my immediate checklist of to-dos and pushing all thoughts of my wild night with Amanda as far from my mind as possible.

For now.

I don't know how she did it, but Rory, Carissa, and Charlee's best friend, Jada who flew in a couple days ago with her husband, have turned what was just another stretch of the beach into a beautiful wedding venue. A few chairs sit on each side of the aisle since there won't be many guests attending this event. As it was literally a decision made in the air on the way down here, Milo and Charlee had enough time to call a few close friends and family and that's it. Understandably, not everyone can attend, but the happy couple promised a huge ass party for everyone when we're home.

Palm leaves line the aisle leading to where Milo and Charlee will stand, and I hold a hollowed coconut filled with tropical flower petals to sprinkle around like a badass. The pergola where the happy couple will be standing was rented from the resort and is adorned with white flowy curtains and some flowers, I wouldn't dream of knowing the name of, but they match Rory's dress so I'm guessing it was coordinated on purpose.

Charlee's bridesmaids, Carissa, Rory, and Jada, all found flowy dresses in one of the boutiques down the road and according to the ladies, Charlee lucked out with a dress off the rack at a local bridal shop. I haven't seen her yet but

I have no doubt she'll look beautiful. If there's anything Rory does well, it's plan events like this. Her creative side knows no bounds and she always goes all in. It's one of her biggest strengths.

"Hey Man," Quinton raises his chin as he approaches. "Have you seen Zeke this morning?"

Though we didn't expect to see him here since he originally told us he needed to stay home, Zeke showed up last night with his little girl, Elsie. He looked a bit like death and it's not like we all didn't notice he showed up here without his wife. Something is definitely up between the two of them, but I respect the fact he doesn't want to talk about it around his little girl. Hopefully we'll get something out of him later. It's unlike him to be so down.

I shake my head. "No, not yet. Hey, what do you suppose happened to him? You think he and Lori are fighting?"

"They have to be, right?" He shrugs. "Why else would he have Elsie with him in Key West?"

"Yeah, true."

Rory steps out to the patio followed by Hawken, Colby, and Milo. "Alright guys, are you about ready to get this shindig started?"

We all nod at the same time Zeke steps out a different door carrying Elsie to a seat in the sand.

I turn to Milo. "What's going on there? Did he say?"

Milo nods. "Lori left him."

Quinton, Hawken, and I gasp. "What the fuck? Are you serious?"

"Mhmm," he says with his hands shoved into his pock-

33

ets. "And when I say she left, I'm pretty sure she left both of them."

"What the actual fuck?" Rory is the one shocked this time. "She left her kid?"

"That's how Zeke made it sound but don't hold me to that. I could be wrong. He didn't go into details because there were people around but long story short, Lori's gone and he's in charge of Elsie now."

"Oh God, poor Zeke."

"Yeah," Milo says as we all watch the two of them from afar.

Rory claps her hands and shakes her head. "But hey! We're here for Milo and Charlee and let me tell you, Charlee looks hot as fuck, so let's get this party started and liven this place up a bit, huh?"

All of us follow suit clapping Milo on the shoulder. "Let's get you your girl, Landric."

"Hell yeah." Milo smiles. "That's a great idea."

Milo and the rest of the guys make their way to the pergola, but I stay behind with my coconut of flower petals watching Zeke and Elsie and feeling bad that he's not up there with the rest of them.

Rory has a staffer start the music and the ladies make their way down the aisle one at a time, Carissa first, followed by Rory and then Jada. And then it's my turn.

Proudly holding my coconut, I wait until the music changes and happily sprinkle flower petals into the air until I reach Zeke and Elsie. I hold my hands out for Elsie in hopes she'll come with me.

"Hey princess, you want to help Uncle Dex?"

Zeke gives me a questioning look and I gesture up

front. "You belong up there, man. Elsie and I have a job to do and so do you."

"What are you talking about? I'm not dressed for this."

"Bullshit. Since when has that stopped any of us? We're family. We stick together and we stand with each other." I turn to look at Milo and he nods, gesturing for Zeke to join them. Elsie moves happily to my strong arms and I let her hold the coconut with my help. Zeke steps down the aisle to join the guys, hugging Milo and bumping fists with the other guys while Elsie and I fight the wind as we playfully toss our flower petals.

Once down the aisle, I help Elsie give everyone a fist bump and then keep her in my arms while we stand next to her dad.

Charlee rounds the corner as the music changes once again for her entrance and damn, Rory wasn't lying when she said Charlee looks hot as fuck. She's an absolute knockout and glancing over at Milo and watching the tears building in his eyes, I'm certain he agrees. Charlee's white dress is long and flowy with a huge slit up the side all the way to her hip and a deep V-neck halter-like top. Her dark hair is half up and half down, just enough to show off her neck but not blow around in her face. She walks barefoot through the sand with a smile on her face bigger than I've ever seen and she has us all following suit.

I may not be the marrying type, but I'm still a bit of a sap when it comes to the happiness of my friends, and I could not be prouder of my friend Milo.

SUSAN RENEE

"Hey."

I turn my head and pass a friendly smile to the woman next to me at the bar who is literally wearing a teeny yellow polka dot bikini, her suntanned skin making the bright color pop. Her long black hair is piled in a bun at the top of her head, her sunglasses resting above her forehead.

Yep. Totally my type.

I'd do her.

"Hi."

"Was that you at the wedding today? With the flowers and the little girl? My friends and I were watching from the pool."

"Yep." I nod. "That was me. One of my buddies got married today."

Her eyes float down my naked torso to my swim trunks and back up. "Well congratulations to your friend. You looked great up there doing your flower guy thing. It was... sexy."

She winks and I know exactly where this is going.

Look all you want, Sweetheart.

Not the first time. Won't be the last.

"Thanks."

"Your wife is a lucky lady."

"She would be if I had one, yes."

"You're not married?"

"Nope."

"How is that even possible?"

"Easy." I shrug. "I don't like to commit."

"Well, how perfect is that then? Neither do I." She slides her hand over my arm resting on the bar. "I'm

Catalina. What do you say we keep each other company tonight? You know, in that perfectly noncommittal way."

I don't even have to look at her to know she's nowhere near what I had with Amanda last night and something about that rubs me the wrong way. If she were Amanda offering herself up to me again, I would be naked in my room and on my knees licking her sweet pussy already, but Catalina is not my Amanda Hugginkis.

The bartender finally hands me my drink which I tip to my mouth before answering the pretty lady in the sexy yellow bikini.

"Catalina, it's a pleasure to meet you, Sweetheart, but I think I'm going to have to take a rain check."

Wow.

Any other day and in any other town I would be taking her up on her offer, bending her over a bed and plowing into her until I can't see straight.

What the hell am I doing?

"Your loss, big guy," she retorts with a disappointed half smile.

"Agreed." I gesture to the bartender and tell him to put Catalina's drink on my tab as well as a free drink for her friends. Fuck, I never do shit like this either, buying women pity drinks.

What the fuck is wrong with me?

"Cannon baaaaall!" Colby pulls his knees to his chest, bounding from the side of the pool into the water. His sheer

37

size guarantees we're all in the splash zone, like it or not. He springs to the surface and grabs his wife who squeals loudly. Zeke's little one, Elsie, mimics her squeal and giggles with laughter, in turn making us all laugh right along with her.

What is it about kid giggles?

Works on adults every time.

Rory and Jada take Elsie from Zeke and play with her in the baby pool splash zone while the rest of us are hanging in the deep end sans the newlyweds. They're not leaving Key West for an official honeymoon right now, but we left them alone for the night once dinner was over.

"What do you suppose they're doin' up there?" Quinton smirks.

I chuckle. "I wonder if she made him wear his cock ring all day?"

The group laughs with me over the memory of Charlee gifting Milo a remote-controlled cock ring for his birthday. Unbeknownst to him, she invited all of us to hang out and then tortured him with it all evening until he couldn't take it anymore. Pretty sure they had it out in the wine closet of his penthouse. Funniest evening ever.

"Either she didn't, or he's gotten really good at withstanding it." Carissa giggles in Colby's arms. "He didn't seem to be squirming up there while they were saying their vows."

"Speaking of squirming, bro..." Hawken gives me some side-eye. "What happened last night after Rory and I went to play pool? Because I came back for you and you were nowhere to be seen."

"Oooh that's my cue to leave." Carissa scrunches her

face. "Y'all do your man-talk thing. I'm gonna go play with Elsie."

"You finally get some action last night, Dex?" Colby asks, watching his wife hop out of the pool and adjust her bikini.

Hawken laughs. "Either he did or he spent the night spread eagle with himself because that's what I walked in on this morning."

"Oh damn." Quinton laughs.

I hadn't thought about her for most of the day, but suddenly all the memories of last night with Amanda wash over me.

"She told me her name was Amanda. Amanda Hugginkis"

The guys burst out laughing. "No, she did not." Quinton cackles. "And you fell for that?"

"Not at all. I played along and told her my name was Ben Dover and by God, I think she may have been the best sex I have ever had."

Colby's brows shoot up. "Wow. That's sayin' something. You sure about that? You have a lot of sex, man."

I nod. "I do and rarely with the same girl twice but I'll tell you what, if Amanda Hugginkis were still here right now, she'd be at my side. Better yet, she'd be *on* her side and I'd be eight inches deep inside her because fuck me...she was..." I shake my head, thoughts of her finger pushing into me, pleasuring me in a way nobody ever has, render me speechless. "She was...shit, I don't even know what to say."

"Where is she now?" Zeke asks.

"She left me sometime last night and had an early morning flight back to Michigan. That's where she's from."

"Does she follow hockey? Did she know who you were?"

I shake my head. "If she does, she didn't lead on that she knew me. Even if she is a hockey fan, she's probably a Detroit fan so maybe she wouldn't know who I am anyway."

"And you didn't think to get her number? I mean, you two could've met up whenever we're in Detroit."

I shake my head. "Nah. You guys know I don't sleep with the same woman twice. The minute I start that shit they'll be crying about relationships and the press will have a field day."

"Well..." Colby claps me on the shoulder. "Good for you for scoring. You needed that."

"Yeah, he did." Hawken nudges me with this shoulder. "He was a grump and a half these past couple days."

"Yeah, yeah. Fuck you too, Hawk. I could've had someone again tonight. Did you see that woman in the yellow bikini?"

The guys look around until they spot her by the bar.

"She propositioned me when I went up to get my beer and I turned her down."

Hawk's eyes bulge. "You turned her down?"

"She's hot man," Quinton murmurs. "Did she have bad teeth or what?"

I laugh. "No. Her teeth were perfectly fine. She just wasn't Amanda."

Holy fuck.

I said that so matter-of-factly I didn't even consider what I was saying.

"Wait." Colby shakes his head. "You just turned down

another night of sex because of the woman you fucked last night?"

I mean...he's right, right?

That's why I turned down Catalina.

Because she's not Amanda.

Slowly, I nod. "I...yeah. I guess so."

"Fuck, man." Hawk shakes his head scoffing out a laugh. "You must've had some night last night."

I told her I would ruin her for any guy who came after me, but what if she ruined me for all future women?

Fuck me.

4

TATUM

AUGUST

My stomach has been queasy for the last several days and today is no better. I didn't think I would be this nervous starting a new job, but apparently, I am. It's not like I don't know what I'm doing. And it's not like I'm feeling overwhelmed with life. I gave myself plenty of time to find a new place, move in, get myself settled, and learn my way around before this day came. That way I could ensure I wouldn't be adding to my stress level by not knowing how to get whatever I might need.

The girl sitting next to me leans over. "First year here?"

"Yeah," I chuckle. "Am I that obvious?"

"No. Not at all. You just weren't shooting the shit with other people in the room, so I assumed you didn't know anybody."

"Ah. You would be correct."

"I'm Nina," she tells me.

"Tate. Well, Tatum, but everyone calls me Tate."

"Nice to meet you, Tate."

"Pleasure to meet you, Nina. What grade?"

"First."

My brows shoot up. "Oh perfect. We'll be first grade friends."

She lifts her hand and I give her a high five just as a petite woman stands in the front of the room.

"Welcome back teachers! I trust you all had a wonderful summer break and are feeling refreshed and ready to hit the ground running in a new school year."

As I look around the library where all the staff are seated, I can probably guess how many of these teachers are veterans with only a few years left and which are brand new to their jobs and not just because some look older than others. The veterans try hard not to roll their eyes at the thought of having to return to work after another wonderful summer break and the newbies of the group are on the edge of their seats with a notebook and pen handy, ready to take on the world one student at a time.

I consider myself to be in between those two groups. Not a first year-teacher as this is technically my ninth year in the field of education, however, this is my first year at Riverside Elementary School. It's my first year working outside the state of Michigan. And it's my first year in a job as a single woman.

New home.

New job.

New me.

That was the plan once my divorce was final. I needed a change. A big change. I didn't want to be someone who got stuck in her hometown for the rest of her life. I wanted to see more of my world. I wanted to meet new people. I wanted to have new life experiences.

So here I am.

From small town Michigan to the Windy City of Illinois, everything about me is different now. I'm ready for a new year with new students. I'm ready to spend my days developing the minds of young first graders and my nights exploring my new environment. I'm excited to meet new friends and hopefully have an active social life. Heck, maybe I can even get involved in some sort of club or charitable organization. The sky's the limit!

The principal, Mrs. Charbly, stands at the front of the room with a small clicker in hand, ready to begin her power point presentation. "If I can have your attention for just a few moments before you disperse to your rooms to work, I want to go over a few new things happening this school year. But before I do that," she smiles, "I'd like for everyone to introduce themselves quickly as we do have several new faces with us this year. Those of you who are new to the district, I'll also introduce you to your mentor teacher for the year."

Each of the teachers before me stands when it's their turn and gives their name, how many years they've been teaching and what grade they teach this year, so when it gets to be my turn, I know exactly what to do.

"Hello. I'm Tate Lowe, new to the district this year. New to the state, actually. This will be my tenth year as an elementary teacher, but my first working here."

"Welcome Ms. Lowe. And your mentor teacher for the year is..." She checks her spreadsheet. "Ms. Foster."

A friendly woman who looks to be about my age if not a

little younger seated at the table next to me waves her hand. "That's me." She leans over the table and whispers, "We'll talk after this."

I give her a confident smile. "Sounds good."

Once it gets around to her, my new mentor stands to introduce herself and I commit her words to my memory so I don't have to ask her name again later.

"Hi." She smiles. "I'm Rory Foster. This is my sixth-year teaching kindergarten right here at Riverside Elementary School."

Rory Foster.

Sixth year.

Kindergarten.

Not much different from me!

"Fantastic." Mrs. Charbly beams. "It's great to see so many smiling faces this morning. We've done so much these past couple months to prepare you all for a strong year, so allow me to go over a few key points with you."

"So, we'll spend some time together here in the next couple of weeks and go over your goals for the year and your instruction plan. It's all pretty simple, really," Rory explains. "Probably even more so for you, Tate, since you've taught before. You know how to do all this stuff. It'll just be making sure everything complies to Illinois state standards in case for some reason there are big discrepancies between here and where you used to teach."

"Sounds great. I can't wait."

"What else can we help you guys with as you prepare for the year?" another teacher seated at our lunch table asks those of us who are new to the district. My new friend Nina and I have gotten along very well this morning. I can tell she'll be a great working partner and I'm already excited to plan out our lessons together. Her mentor teacher's name is Shelly who seems to also be friends with my mentor, Rory.

"You guys have been so helpful all morning. Really," I tell them. "Even knowing where to go to grab the best cup of coffee or sandwich at lunchtime is a huge help. But also thank you for pointing out which die-cut machine works best. God knows I'll spend hours in front of that thing."

Nina puts her hand on mine. "Girl, same. My wheels have been turning ever since I saw plans for butterfly life stages and the hatching of baby chicks in the spring. Oh, the fun we can have with craft time, am I right?"

"Totally," I cringe. "But I should tell you now, I'm a little bit of a glitter whore. I'm a sucker for all things sparkly."

Rory gives me an excited high five. "YAAASS QUEEN! We are all about the sparkle in our hallway!" She lowers her voice as if she's sharing a secret. "Also, it makes me laugh every time we do a glitter craft and I get to send my kiddos home with glitter and glue everywhere. The moms probably secretly hate me, but I just smile and wave. It's amazing."

My stomach lurches at the thought of glue. Just thinking about the smell of glue right now makes me nauseous. "Oh, my God, the smell of glue could make me gag right now and I have no idea why, but also, you guys are so my kind of people." I beam. "I seriously am so pumped to start this year. I'm hungry for it."

"Speaking of hungry, you're going to work up an appetite for sure." Shelly gestures to my Ziplock back of goldfish I've been munching on. "You're going to need a bigger lunch than that."

Rory takes note of my snack lunch. "Truth." She pops a grape into her mouth. "If you need a sandwich shop or fast-food recommendation, I'm happy to point them out. Oh, and there's always a microwave and fridge here so don't hesitate to bring leftovers."

"Oh, trust me, I love to cook and I usually eat more than this. My stomach has just been in knots the last few days and for whatever reason these stupid little fish are the only things that don't make me nauseous."

Nina's brow furrows. "Uh oh. What's that about?"

"Probably just nerves. First time moving away from my hometown. New home. New job. Once my divorce was finalized, I wanted to make some big changes and I did, soooo, I think I'm just settling in, you know?"

Shelly shrugs. "Or you're pregnant."

All heads turn to me and then back to Shelly.

"What?" She lifts her shoulder again. "When I was pregnant with my son, Zander, I couldn't have their home-made slime in my house because the smell alone made me vomit. And I ate goldfish crackers like my life depended on it. There was always a bag in my purse."

"I remember that," Rory exclaims with a chuckle. "I used to raid your stash whenever I was hungry.

"Bitch." Shelly winks. "Who steals a pregnant woman's snacks? Only you, that's who."

"Sorry not sorry. You didn't gain a ton of baby weight so you're welcome."

As the ladies are talking, I'm rolling back through details of the last couple months in my head.

When was my last period?

I can't even remember.

I can't be pregnant.

Not possible.

Right? Like, it can't be possible.

Last person I slept with?

Haven't slept with Michael in over a year.

Haven't slept with anyone el...wait.

Key West.

Ben Dover.

Could it be?

Have I had a period since then?

He wore a condom, didn't he?

I'm nearly certain.

I don't think I've had a period since before Key West.

He's the only one I've been with since my divorce.

If I'm pregnant...oh shit.

Shit. Shit. Shit.

Fuck.

Dammit.

Hell.

"Hey, you okay?" Nina shakes me from my inner thoughts. "Your face is white." Shelly and Rory turn their attention to me as well.

"Shit, Nina's right. You do look a little pale, Tate." Rory touches my forehead like a mom checking her kid. "No fever though."

My stomach churns and I know I'm about to be sick. There isn't even time for me to run so I'm more than grateful when Shelly reacts swiftly, grabbing a small trash can and shoving it in front of me. I turn my head away from the table and lose all the goldfish I had just eaten along with the saltines I had for breakfast.

"Maybe it's the flu," I hear Rory suggest.

"Not the flu." Shelly shakes her head. "I would bet anything." She eyes me across the table as she sips her water. "Is it possible?"

Swallowing the huge uncomfortable knot in my throat, I nod. "I guess it's...possible."

Shelly winks, a knowing smirk crawling across her face. "I knew it. I've been pregnant enough times to recognize it anywhere."

Rory's eyes grow and her jaw drops. "Oh, my God Tate! You're pregnant?" she coos. "Oh, my God this will be so much fun! I'll be the best honorary aunt this kid has ever known."

Tears spring to my eyes and they're anything but happy ones. Holding my head in my hand I murmur, "How could this have happened?"

"Must've been some big dick energy, am I right?" Shelly asks.

I look around at my new friends and suddenly I want to crawl into a hole and stay there for the rest of my days. This was not what I had in mind when I set out for a new job and a new home and a new me. I wanted big changes, yes, but not like this. How am I supposed to do this all on my own?

"Who was it? Do you know the guy?" Rory asks.

I shake my head, embarrassed at what I'm about to admit. "Just some guy I hooked up with on vacation. I didn't even know his name."

"Oooh," Nina swoons. "So, it *was* some big dick energy."

I nod slowly remembering the way he made me feel that night.

The multiple orgasms he gifted me.

The way he came when I touched him.

Pleasured him.

His sweet demeanor afterward.

"It was..." I sigh. "It was an amazing night, and one I've thought about often."

"Did he wear a condom? Have you been with anyone else?"

"He did wear a condom and no. There's been nobody else. Not before, not after."

"So. If you are pregnant, there's no doubt it's his."

"No doubt." I shake my head bewildered. "I just can't believe we never talked about where we were from. I mean I told him I was moving from Michigan but I don't think I ever mentioned where I was moving to, and he never spoke a word of where he was from. Florida is filled with a shit ton of people. He could be anybody anywhere." I squeeze my eyes closed. "What the hell am I going to do?"

Rory tenderly grips my arm. "First of all, you're going to take a deep breath. This could be something or it could be nothing. You won't know until you test."

"Yeah." I nod. "True."

"And if it's positive, Shelly and I will make sure you get

into a good doctor because prenatal care is important and you shouldn't wait. How long ago was vacation?"

"Uh, a couple months. Mid-May.

"Okay so you could potentially be..." Rory counts in her head. "Ten to twelve weeks?"

"Shit. Yeah, I guess so?"

This knowledge isn't making me feel any better. Have I seriously been pregnant all summer and just didn't know it?

"God, how could I be so stupid?" I lay my head in my palm.

"You're not stupid, Tate. Sometimes women have no idea they're pregnant. Some women don't get the same symptoms. Or maybe you're not pregnant at all. You want some company when you take the test this evening? I'm more than willing to be there for moral support."

Nina raises her hand. "Me too."

"I'm sorry but I already have rugrats I have to pick up at daycare after work." Shelly frowns. "But I'll be there in spirit."

"Thanks ladies, but I think I can manage it alone."

"Okay, but you know we're going to be sitting by our phones, right? You had better keep us posted!"

"I promise as soon as I know, you'll know."

Rory takes my hand. "You're going to be okay, Tate. I promise."

"I seriously don't know what I would do without you ladies. Is it weird to say this has been singularly one of the most frightening days of my life?"

"This is nothin', sweetheart." Shelly waves her hand. "Wait till you have to push a nine-pound watermelon out of that pretty little cooch with no drugs because you dilated too fast."

Rory looks at her friend with wide eyes. "Not helping Shell."

She cringes. "Oh, sorry. You'll be fine. Really."

I'm fucked.

So totally fucked.

5

DEX

"What...in the..." Rory stops in her tracks as she walks through the door. "What are you doing?"

Pass second stitch over the first...

"What's it look like I'm doing? I told you I was learning to knit."

She cackles. "You? Knit?"

"Yeah. What's the big deal?" My tongue pokes out the side of my mouth as I wrap my yarn around the needle counterclockwise and then pull it through the first loop, guiding it with my index finger. "It's supposed to be relaxing. Hawk's brother knits. Did you know that? Anyway, he told me it might help me with my restlessness."

Whatever has been going on with me this summer, it's been driving me up a fucking wall. I find myself bored and moody more often than not, even when I have an open schedule and plenty of money to do whatever the hell I want. Nothing I consider sounds intriguing to me. The only thing I've spent more than ten minutes contemplating is the idea of driving to Michigan and searching for the one person I know who lives there.

Amanda.

Hell, I don't even know her real name.

The woman in the black bikini.

The woman who touched me in ways no one ever has.

The woman who made me come harder than I ever have in my life.

The woman I haven't stopped thinking about since the night we spent together in Key West.

She was celebrating all things new in her life and her confidence and bravery were attractive as hell.

She was without a doubt the best sex I've ever had.

Rory hangs her purse on the hook by the door and drops her teacher bag on the floor and then crosses the room to sit next to me, eyeing my every move. "Where did you even learn to do that?"

"YouTube."

"Are you serious?"

I take my eyes off my needles momentarily to look at her. "Yeah. Why?"

"Like, did you actually walk yourself into a craft store to buy that yarn?"

"Fuck no." Now it's my turn to laugh. "I might have mentioned to Mrs. Pinkle the other day when I ran into her in the elevator that I thought about learning to knit and she showed up the next day with everything I needed and offered to give me a lesson."

She chuckles. "You're shitting me."

"I totally shit you not," I smile right along with her.

"You better watch out for dear old Mrs. Pinkle, Dexter. I think she has a crush on you."

"Nah, she's just lonely. I try to say hello whenever I see her."

"Pffft. She's not lonely." Rory lifts herself from the oversized couch and crosses over to the kitchen to open the fridge. "She has like what, four corgis now? She hired a professional dog walker you know. God, if she spoke with a British accent, I may very well think she's the Queen. Hey what do you want for dinner?"

"What are you makin'?" I smirk again but I keep my eyes on my hands, so I don't mess up my gorgeous ten rows of knitting. Rory doesn't always cook meals around here, nor do I expect her to, especially in the off season when I'm more than capable. She does usually help me out during the season though when she knows I carry a demanding schedule, but now that she's back to school and I'm just starting preseason conditioning, I try to ease a little of the household burden and do more around our condo.

Maybe it's weird that we're still living together after all these years, but I know she doesn't make a ton of money as an elementary school teacher and I make more than I need, so I've always taken it upon myself to take care of her. I may only be a few years older than my little sister, but I was there for her when our parents weren't. We're bonded and until one of us finds someone to settle down with, and I don't see that happening anytime soon, I figure I may as well let her save as much money as she can since I can afford for us to live in a nice place.

It's the least I can do.

"I'm just kidding, by the way," I tell her. "I ordered from Wong's."

She shuts the fridge and turns to look at me, her eyes wide. "Did you get the egg rolls?"

"Did I get the eggrolls," I murmur. "Of course, I got the egg rolls. In fact, I got you four egg rolls. And had to tell Mr. Wong himself about your obsession."

"You did not!" She laughs and runs over to throw her arms around my neck, kissing the top of my head. "Just what I was craving. Thank you!"

Rory's phone dings in her pocket so she pulls it out to look at it and gasps.

"She's really pregnant! Oh, my gosh."

"What?" My head snaps up. "Who's pregnant? Charlee? Smallson? Why didn't they tell us?"

"No, no. Her name is Tate. She's one of my newest school friends. I'm her mentor this year."

"Oh gotcha. Okay. I don't have to care about that, right?"

"Have you fucked Tate or any of my other friends lately?"

I raise my eyes from my knitting just enough to give her a displeased look. "You know, contrary to what you must believe, I don't fuck every woman I meet."

"Well, that's relatively good to know. So, no. You don't know her. Will probably never meet her. And now that she's pregnant if you ever *do* meet her, you won't bother trying to fuck her so nope. You're safe. Anyway, that's who the text was from. She was going to test when she got home. I guess it's positive. Poor thing. She's new in town. Doesn't have anyone here."

"She's not married?"

"Nope."

"Boyfriend?"

"Don't think so."

"Hmm. That sucks for her," I state as I knit my twelfth row. "Tell her not to worry. You're now invested and will be the best damn Auntie Rory her little kid has ever had."

She giggles, but she knows I'm right. "You're right. I love kids. What can I say?"

"You'll have that child singing those Go-Noodle songs before it can walk. I swear if I have to hear shit about all the eggs being broken and pepperoni pizzas one more time, I'm going to stick these needles in my ears and puncture my own ear drums."

She cackles this time. "You know me so well."

DING DONG.

"That'll be dinner."

Rory gets up to answer the door. "So, what are you making with all that yarn, exactly?"

Hmm. I never really thought about what I would actually make with this knitting project.

A pair of socks?

A sweater?

Nah. Way too complicated.

A scarf maybe?

"I guess I'm making a baby blanket."

Yeah, that should be easy enough.

I tap a few buttons on the treadmill, increasing my speed, welcoming the sweat as it drips from my body. With the official start of preseason coming next month, I've upped my conditioning game in order to be in my best shape. This year, we're bringing home the fucking cup if it kills me. If that means picking up an extra workout throughout the week, so be it. It's good for my mindset right now anyway.

I've had way more pent-up energy this summer than I remember having before. I've done a slow jog if not a full four and a half mile run every day. That coupled with my strength training is hell on my body but it's still not enough to settle my mind. I took up knitting because Hawk noticed I've been irritable since getting back from Key West and thought maybe keeping my hands and brain busy creating something would help. Even Rory accused me of man-struating on a few occasions, which only pissed me off even more.

"Welcome to my life," is all my little sister had to say to me.

Admittedly, it's getting annoying, even for myself, and at this point, I feel like I've tried everything I can do to release the tension.

That's not true.

I haven't tried everything.

But that's only because for the first time in my adult life, the interest just isn't there.

It's not like women haven't tried to get me to sleep with them in the past couple months. Hell, I even found myself lip locked with some chick at the bar a couple weeks ago, but I didn't feel a fucking thing and my cock wasn't interested.

When the treadmill beeps, I lower my speed and jog out the rest of my workout, finally coming to stop and grabbing the t-shirt hanging on the bar to dry my face.

Hawken lowers the barbells in his hands and looks up at me from his bench. "Still that bad, huh?"

Drying the sweat from my face, I toss my shirt next to my water bottle. "If I don't figure my shit out quick, this is going to be fucking hell of a season and Coach is going to chop my sad lonely dick right off so I stop worrying about it."

"Is that really your concern? Where all this pent-up energy is coming from? Because you can't get laid?"

If Hawken wasn't my best friend, I might've punched him in the nuts just now.

"Dude, it's not that I can't get laid. It's that I have zero interest in even pursuing it."

Hawk cocks his head. "Since when does Dex Foster not want to get laid?"

I plop down on one of the workout benches near him. "Right? Believe me, I've been asking myself that for months now. But ever since Key West the interest is gone. So, what the fuck is wrong with me? Why isn't my dick working for me anymore?"

His brows shoot up. "You mean it's seriously not working? Like, not even for you?"

I roll my eyes. "Okay, okay, it works for me, alright? But even that...Fuck, I use to jack off every damn day, but now? Even my fist doesn't sound appealing."

"That's a hell of a cock block, Dex."

"Fuckin' right it is. Now how do I get rid of it?"

He shakes his head. "I don't know, Bro. This is still about the girl, right? The girl from Key West?"

"Amanda."

"Amanda," he repeats with a laugh. "Amanda Hugginkis. I remember. Dude, I've never seen you hung up on a woman before."

"Trust me. I've never *been* hung up on a woman before."

And that's the truth. I'm always the one and done guy. The one who gets what he wants from the lady he's with and then easily sends her on her way. Though, for some weird reason, I never thought about sending Amanda away. Once she sucked me off and gave me an orgasm so intense, I damn near forgot where I was, I wanted her to stay. I wanted more of her. I wanted to experience all I could before she ended up nothing but a happy dream. I wanted to bottle her up and save her. Like my own genie in a bottle.

I don't do relationships, but I happily would've done Amanda—or whatever her name really is, again and again, and again had I not fucking fallen asleep. Never in my life have I come across a woman who had no inhibitions when it came to being heard or pleasured but then also gave it right back. Sure, women always want to suck my dick, but I've always justified their actions with the thought that they just want to be able to say they've sucked off a famous hockey player.

But Amanda had no idea who I was.

She agreed to a night of orgasms *for her*.

A night of pleasure *for her*.

Neither of us ever said a damn thing about me.

But she gave the pleasure right back. Willingly.

And that meant something to me.

I can't put words to it, but it fucking meant something.

"Maybe you need to find her. Maybe have one more go with her and see if it helps."

"And how the fuck am I supposed to find a woman named Amanda Hugginkis who lives in Michigan? That's an impossible task since it's not even her real name and trust me, I've looked. Every profile I come across ends up being for some drag queen somewhere. Did you know there are seventy Amanda Hugginkises on just one social media platform? If she's on social media at all, she clearly doesn't go by that name. She never told me her real name or where in Michigan she lives. And come to think of it, she told me she interviewed for a job in a new town so who knows if she A – got the job, and B – had to move to said new town to take the job. I basically don't know shit about her except that teaches first grade."

Quinton saunters into the gym, setting his water bottle on one of the shelves just inside the door.

"What's up fuckers?"

"Just trying to help Foster here figure out why his dick is on strike."

"Whose dick is on strike?" Colby asks as he follows behind Quinton.

"Foster's."

"What's up, Foster? You need a wingman or just a pretty fluffer?"

"No, I don't need a wingman. I just need—"

"The mystery woman from Key West," Hawk finishes my sentence. "That's who he needs. Apparently, she broke his dick."

"The one-night stand?" Colby's brows lift. "You're still on about her?"

"Ugh." I frown. "She didn't break my dick. I think she... I don't know. I think she broke *me*."

Colby smirks. "Awww I think Dexter has a crush!"

"Shut the fuck up, Nelson."

Colby laughs. "You know we love you man. But seriously, it's been what? Two, almost three months?"

"Yeah."

"That's a long time for you."

"Tell me something I don't know. I'm starting to feel like a fucking priest." It's not like my frustration has stayed locked up good and tight inside. The whole team has seen my mood swings these past couple months.

"Taking any supplements you've never taken before?"

I shake my head. "Nope."

"Have you had your testosterone checked?" Quinton asks me.

"I get physicals just as regularly as you all do. Everything has been squeaky clean."

"So, what can we do to help? You need to go out tonight? You want to bypass Pringle's and look somewhere else? You need some fresh porn to open you up? What?"

Pringle's Pub is the one place in town that always provides the team a safe place to hang out where we can be undisturbed most of the time. They've always treated us like royalty because we bring them so much business, especially during the regular season. It's also the place I've easily been able to pick up women. All the single ladies know the team hangs out there regularly so there's never a shortage of willing puck bunnies.

But I simply have no appetite for any of them.

"Nah. It's fine. I'll figure it out eventually." I pick up my water bottle and chug half of it and then grab my sweaty t-shirt. "Thanks though. I've gotta hit the showers."

Hawk claps my shoulder as I pass by him. "Hey don't worry man. You'll get your mojo back. I'm sure of it."

Someone tell that to my dick.

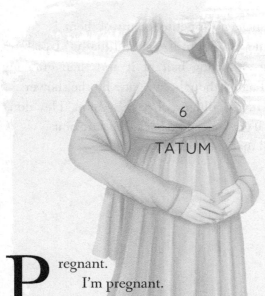

6

TATUM

Pregnant.

I'm pregnant.

Four tests last night and six new ones this morning and every single one of them says the same thing.

I have less than nine months to figure out how the hell I'm going to handle this newfound situation. Before I do anything else I run to the calendar hanging on my fridge and count back. I was with the mystery man also known as Ben Dover in May, which should put me at, "Eleven weeks? How the hell did I not know for eleven weeks? Shit." It also means this baby will be here by the end of February or beginning of March.

Slowly, I back up and stumble into one of my two kitchen chairs. I don't even have a reason to own two kitchen chairs except the table came with two chairs so here I am with an empty seat next to me. Like this table knew one day I was going to need a second chair and now look at me.

"Eleven weeks."

How could this even be?

I watched him put that condom on.

Did it break and he didn't tell me?

Is he that kind of guy?

How would I know? I barely knew him.

Sighing in my chair, I know in the grand scheme of things, I can question all I want, but it changes nothing.

I am now a future single mother.

My baby will never know its father...because I don't even know its father.

"How could I have been so stupid?"

Instinctively, I lower my hand to my stomach. I'm not a skinny rail so I wonder if it's possible I might look pregnant to someone if I were naked. I don't feel like I look different, but I would be lying if I said I didn't feel any different.

In hindsight, I've been ignoring symptoms for a while now. Not on purpose, obviously, but had I really been paying attention, maybe I would've caught this earlier. I was super tired for much of June but I chalked that up to having to move to a new town and getting situated. I've been nauseous for at least the last three weeks assuming it was new job, new town, new life nerves. And my boobs... yep. They've been busting out of my bras a bit but once again, I knew I had been eating more fast food than usual as I was getting all my stuff moved and organized. I was giving myself a little grace until the school year started.

Tears spring to my eyes as worry and fear set in. I knew I was strong enough to finally walk away from my lying, cheating ex. I knew I was strong enough to move to a new town and start a new job. But this...

I'm not sure I'm strong enough for this.

"What am I going to do?" After navigating through an entire morning of teacher training that included emergency scenarios like intruders in the building, school shootings, and natural disasters, my brain is overloaded. All I could think about while watching those training videos was what I would do if my own kid had to experience any of these moments.

What if I can't get to them?

How do I keep them safe?

How do I send them off to school feeling safe when in reality, I'll fear for their safety every day?

The water works explode the minute my butt hits the chair at my lunch table, my three new friends watching and waiting for what I might have to say.

"I'm really sorry I'm having a weak moment right now, you guys, but I need a quick pity party for just a few minutes." I bow my head into my hands and allow myself to cry out my fears and frustrations.

"Let it out, Tate." Rory pats my shoulder. "Even Shelly here remembers what it was like to be pregnant for the first time. It's exciting and scary all at the same time."

I lift my head. "When does the exciting part start? Because the last twenty-four hours have been nothing but a horribly bad dream that I wish I could wake up from and never dream again."

Shelly crunches down on an apple. "Listen, the exciting part comes at the end when you're finally holding that little bundle of joy that destroys your body and your mind and your heart in your hands. The little miracle that you grew all by yourself." She points to my stomach. "That little one in there will know nothing of your fears and inhibitions because the moment he or she comes into this world, they will have eyes for nobody else but you. And you'll fall in love so hard, you'll forget every sad and scary moment you ever had during these next few months. That's the exciting part."

I blow out a staggered breath. "You make it all sound so wonderful, Shelly."

"Yeah, yeah. I won't mention what happens when that kid's head rips your lady bits apart on its evacuation or the sleepless nights you'll have for weeks at a time. Or how hard and painful your nipples will—"

"I think she gets it, Shell." Rory shakes her head, giving Shelly that face that says shut the fuck up.

Pushing my fingers through my hair, I comb a few layers away from my face. "Like, who even lives this kind of life? How did I get here? In the past four months, I have officially divorced my husband, interviewed for a new job, gone on vacation to celebrate my divorce and new job, had the best sex I have seriously ever had with a man I don't even know, and now I'm pregnant with his kid and will never be able to tell him about it. And now my kid will never know its father." *Sniffle.* "What the ever-loving hell did I do to deserve this?"

A sympathetic smile tugs at the corner of Nina's lips. "You know, if my mom were here right now, she would probably say you're looking at things all wrong."

"All wrong? Nothing is going right!"

She shakes her head. "But that's where you're wrong.

You left a deceitful, selfish, unloving man, you not only interviewed but were granted a new job, you moved yourself to a new town, met three new pretty fantastic friends if I do say so myself..."

"Agreed." Rory winks.

"And you were granted the opportunity to bring a child into this world as a loving, caring, compassionate mother. Did you not want kids?"

"Of course, I wanted kids. I just..." I slouch in my chair, releasing a heavy sigh. "This just wasn't how I pictured it."

"Is any of the last four months how you pictured it though?" she asks me. "Did you wake up even a year ago and say, 'I think today I will divorce my husband, go on vacation, fuck a hot guy, and carry his child all while starting a new job in a new state'?"

Her query makes me chuckle. "Alright, you got me. No, I guess not."

"See? Life isn't something you can plan for," she explains. "Life is an experience. Something you live wholeheartedly and with passion...until you die."

Shelly gestures toward Nina. "Spoken like a true hippie."

"Maybe." Nina shrugs. "My mom was always a very spiritual person. Always told me if I don't choose to get busy living, I may as well get busy dying."

Well, that's a perspective I hadn't considered.

I suppose there's some good truth to that statement.

"Thanks Nina."

"Anytime, babe. I really think you're going to be just fine. And we'll all be here to help you through the next few months. Don't sweat it."

"Do you have family back home?" Rory asks me.

"Yeah. I do. A wonderfully supportive family."

"Have you told any of them yet?"

I shake my head. "No. I need to process this first, you know? Make sure I'm in the right mindset."

"Do you think they'll be supportive of you?"

"They may be a little disappointed or sad that the father isn't in the picture, but I know they'll support me without a doubt. My parents have been there for me every step of the way. They won't shove my fuckups in my face. They saw how broken I was when Michael cheated on me with my best friend."

The ladies gasp and Rory nearly chokes on her water. "Whaaaat? Your best friend?"

I nod.

"Giiirl, no." Shelly waves her hand. "I'm going to tell you what this is because ain't nobody gonna tell my girl, Tate, here, that she fucked up. So, this is how it is."

"Okay..."

"Honey, you left that man and your bitch best friend high and dry and you took yourself out of the equation for good." She gives me a high five.

"Then, like the badass woman you are, you got yourself a brand-new job, and a brand-new home, in a brand-new state all by your fuckin' self. Nobody could do that for you." She points to me. "You did that." She high fives me again.

"Then you took yourself on vacation and had the best fuck of your life with a man who clearly knew how to rock your body in ways your dumbass loser of a husband never did and you enjoyed every fuckin' minute of it, am I right?"

Thoughts of Ben with his hands on my body, his tongue

between my legs, his cock warm in my mouth float through my mind as I nod. "Ooooh yes."

"That's right, girl. You enjoyed it. And now you're carrying this man's baby and you are going to be the best badass mother this kid has ever known and you're going to look at yourself in the mirror every morning and tell yourself how strong you are because you can do all those things. You're a fighter. You're a lover. You're a goddamn over-comer, Tate Lowe. Don't let anyone tell you differently."

Rory and Nina begin a slow clap. "Wow!" Rory says with amusement in her voice. "That was an inspiring speech if I ever heard one."

"Hey, if I don't practice my daily affirmations, I'll die in a sea of needy children," she laughs. "And that is a sad way to die."

Once our laughter dies down, Rory asks about prenatal care. "I don't have a doctor yet. I guess now I need to do some searching."

"Okay." She grabs my hand. "Why don't we get together after our last meeting today and we can talk through everything so your mind isn't a huge blur. How does that sound?"

"Oh, my God, that would be great. Thank you, Rory."

"It's the least I can do. I can go through and show you which doctors the ladies around here prefer, and we can kind of make a plan for the next few months at least, so you're comfortable. We'll need to think about things like maternity leave and plans for when that happens and all that stuff we don't always think about. I'm more than willing to be by your side every step of the way. If you need someone for an appointment, I'm there. You need a Lamaze coach? Count me in. You need me to bitch slap the old woman at the grocery store who thinks she has the right to touch your baby bump? I will bitch slap her all the way to kingdom come."

I squeeze her fingers wrapped around my hand and inhale a deep breath.

I can do this.

I can do hard things.

Everything is going to be fine.

"I like that plan. Let's rip off the Band-Aid, right?"

Rory nods with a smile. "Right."

7
DEX

The team is off to a solid start this season with a standing of 26-04-0 coming into the holiday season. Everyone is healthy, strong, and eager to be on the ice soaking up the energy in the arena. We started out with an undefeated preseason and we aim to keep as close to that streak as possible for as long as we can. We're currently up two to one against Detroit, busting our asses to come out on top again.

"There you go, Thorton! Keep on him!" I shout to one of our rookies from the bench. He's fast and he's clean. An impressive young player who has the drive to work his way to the top. He reminds me a lot of myself when I was just starting out in the league.

"He's good for the team." Colby nods as we watch Thorton do the job we've known for so long. "He'll be a strong defenseman as he gains more experience."

"Thinkin' of retiring old man?"

Colby smirks. "In your dreams, Foster."

"Nah, there's only one person in my dreams lately, Nelson, and you ain't her."

"No shit." He chuckles. "You still hung up on that girl? Your Key West girl?"

"Everyday." My shoulders slump. "Every fucking day." Is it wrong that I'm still infatuated with the woman even after all this time? It's weird, I know. God, I feel like a desperate teenager looking for anyone but my fist to get me off these days, but nobody has come close to Amanda Hugginkis.

Colby cheers for Miller when he blocks Detroit's third attempt at a goal. "Dude, all you've got to do is ask someone else out. It's that easy."

I wince. "It's not that easy though, man."

"Because?"

"Because all I know how to do is fuck, and even that is boring me these days. Nobody is the same and when I'm with someone else, I can't get Key West out of my mind. It's like she lives in my brain rent free and she's taken over my dick with some voodoo type shit."

"Voodoo? Really?" Milo laughs.

"Yes! I swear to God I try as hard as I can and it's not like any woman I'm with isn't enjoyable. A pussy is a pussy but Amanda's pussy was top shelf. Cream of the crop. Premium pussy...and she did things to me..." I shake my head unable to even talk about it or I'll get hard.

Milo stands, preparing to be called in for his next shift with Colby and me.

"I wouldn't worry too much about it. Just let whatever happens, happen. Who knows, maybe some other fine piece of ass will come along and sweep you off your feet."

"Foster! Nelson! Landric! You're in. Let's go!" Coach Denovah shouts down the bench. Colby and I are already sitting on the wall ready to race out onto the ice. Milo is right behind us.

"In the meantime," Colby smirks, "until that happens, that dick of yours is going to need watered, and fed, and told it's pretty at least a few times a week before it shrivels up and dies."

He and Milo laugh as they hit the ice running.

As defensemen, it's our job to protect our goalie and neutralize the offense when they're in our zone. Colby and I could do our jobs in our sleep having played together for years now. We're always laser focused, homing in on the puck, passing back and forth, circling the other team's offense, and distracting them enough to get the puck out of our zone and back down the ice.

In a new play we haven't spent much time on this season, Shay passes the puck to me and I see the opening I need. I sprint down the ice, the puck gliding in front of me as I work my stick to keep it in control. The net gets closer and I know I could shoot it into his five hole and make the goal.

But that's not part of the play.

Instead, I rear back as though I'm about to shoot the goal, and then swiftly pass it back behind me to Malone who circles the net and shoots it back to me. I send a false pass to Landric and before their goalie knows the puck is in my possession, I shoot it into the net to bring our score to three to one.

"Nicely done, Foster!" Shay claps my shoulder as the

rest of the team huddles around me, hugging it out and celebrating our inevitable win.

God, I love this game.

8

TATUM

Laundry doesn't fold itself.

I set the basket of clothes on the coffee table next to me so I don't have to completely bend at the waist to reach for them. At seven months pregnant small tasks like this get harder and harder to do. It was sweet of Rory and the other teachers at the school to hold a baby shower for me before the holiday season got underway. It's given me time to wash as many of these new baby clothes as I can and set up some resemblance of a nursey in my second bedroom. It's a little cramped in there but with it just being the two of us, we don't need much space yet. Picking up the remote I scroll through the random channels on the television looking for something to watch while I fold this laundry.

"Too bad I don't get the Hallmark Channel."

I scroll through several news channels that I have zero interest in watching. News these days just makes me sad and with my hormones as they are, I don't feel like crying over the latest shooting or getting all worked up over politics. I hit an entertainment channel about a day in the life of a Kardashian and roll my eyes. "Nope. Not this either." *Law and Order* is on three channels at the same time and then I come across one of the local stations playing tonight's hockey game against my home team of Detroit. A few of their names I recognize, as my brothers are big hockey fans, so I leave it on as something to absentmindedly listen to while I get work done. I don't know what the Red Tails' record is right now, nor do I pay that much attention to hockey, so who knows, maybe Detroit will win this one.

I'll consider it a nice gift from home.

"Up ahead, Detroit's Yugchenko couldn't get to it, Redtails' Foster and Nelson move to the inside. Foster moves to shoot but passes to Nelson and Foster takes it back," the announcer calls, his energy and excitement building. "It's Foster going in and he stops, locks, and SCOOOOORES and the Red Tails are in the lead three to one!"

"Oooor maybe they won't win tonight. Get your shit together, Detroit!"

I don't know how long I sit here folding clothes before I nod off but when my eyes open again there are two baby onesies on my stomach, the hockey game is over, and the press is in one of the locker rooms holding interviews. They talk to Chicago's team captain, can't quite remember his name, and then move to the next guy.

"Dex Foster, how happy are you with the stats tonight? You had one goal and one assist. Not something you see every day from a defenseman."

"Uh, yeah. I was just thinking there are only two minutes left in the game, we better score so we can keep our lead. I didn't want us going into a tie. It would've been too tight. When Nelson gave me the perfect shot I...you know."

"You made sure to shoot your shot."

As I fold the last two onesies and add them to my pile of clothes, I roll my eyes and snort at the interviewer who just spoke. "You just wanted to say shoot your shot."

Finally, I raise my eyes from what I'm doing to the television, catching sight of the player being interviewed, and freeze. My chest tightens as if all the air has been sucked away and a shocking jolt zips through my whole body.

"Holy fucking shit. It's him." I stare at the television, my jaw nearly unhinged and my heart racing in my chest. "Ben Dover," I whisper. "Is it really...how is this..." I squint hard at the television. "Is this even possible?"

The man I'm staring at is the spitting image of the man I spent a blissful night with in Key West this past summer. The man who gave me multiple orgasms. The man whose child I'll give birth to in just two short months. He's grasping a towel around his neck and his hair is wet. Either he's that sweaty or he just got out of the shower. His eyes though. I would recognize those stormy gray eyes anywhere. And his voice...

"I had no idea you would be this incredibly tight."

"Let me feel this pretty pussy clench around my fingers, and when they do, I'm going to clean you out with my tongue."

It's him.

It has to be.

How do I know for sure?

I grab my phone from the couch beside me and search

his name on the internet. When I click on the image search, I'm rewarded with tons of pictures of the man I one hundred percent recognize as Ben Dover from Key West.

"Dex Foster."

Foster.

Hmm, is it possible there's a relation to Rory?

Nah. I've never heard her talk about him.

Surely if she had a celebrity athlete brother, she would talk about him.

Holy Shit. I can't even believe this is happening.

Dex Foster.

"I slept with Dex Foster of the Chicago Red Tails."

I glance down at my huge baby bump. "Oh, my God I'm having this man's baby and he doesn't even know."

A wave of nausea hits me hard. I high tail it to the bathroom and dry heave into the toilet. My skin breaks out into a sweat and my hands start shaking.

"Oh God. How is this happening?"

I sit on the edge of the shower, my head in my hands. "How the hell am I supposed to tell him?"

No way will he believe me. Fuck, he probably doesn't even remember me. He's a celebrity and I'm just the first-grade teacher he knocked up. Shit. Nobody will believe I word I say. I'll be seen as some crazy lady trying to find my own celebrity status or as someone trying to trick him into money or a relationship. Fucking hell. I don't want that.

My hands on my head, I rock forward and back reminding myself to breathe.

Forward and back.

Breathe.

Forward and back.

Breathe.

What do I do?

How would I even go about telling him if I wanted to? It's not like I can just drop into his DMs and say 'Oh hi, remember me? The girl you fucked in Key West? Hey yeah that was great and now I'm having your kid so...just wanted to let you know'.

Maybe I just don't tell him?

Not right now?

If not now, when?

After the baby is born?

What if I never tell him?

Ugh, and deny this child the right to know his or her father?

What if I tell him and he wants nothing to do with the baby?

What if he offers me money to shut up about it?

Would he do that to his child?

My phone dings with a text in the living room so I calm myself enough to leave the bathroom to see who it's from.

ELIZA

Hey babe! Haven't chatted in a while?
How are you feeling? How's baby?

Yes! Eliza! She's exactly who I need to talk to. She'll tell me what to do.

ME

Call me right fucking now!

I don't even let my phone ring when I see her name appear on my screen.

"Hey."

"Are you okay? Is the baby okay? What can I do? Should I call someone for you? Are you in labor?"

"What? No. I'm fine. Well..." I scoff. "I'm so far from fine, but physically, I'm fine. Baby is fine. What's going on?"

"TATUM! You do NOT text your best friend and tell her to call you ASAP when you're seven months pregnant and could technically go into labor at any time! You scared the bejeesus out of me!"

"Oh. I'm sorry. I didn't mean to scare you, but also, oh, my God, Eliza I need to tell you something and it's a big something and I don't know what the fuck to do about it, so I need you tell me what to do because I am at a complete loss here."

"Okay. Take a breath, Sis. What's going on?"

"Remember Key West?"

"Uh, yeah..." she says.

"Remember the guy? Like, THE GUY?"

She snickers. "Ben Dover? Yeah. You didn't stop talking about him for months. He's the father of your baby. We know this. What about him?"

"Eliza, I know who he is."

She gasps on the other end of the line. "Wait, whaaaat? How do you know who he is? You guys didn't trade real names, right? Isn't that what you said?"

"Yes, that's what I said but I saw him tonight."

"WHAT? In CHICAGO?"

"He's in Chicago, yes, but I saw him on my fucking television because he plays hockey for the Chicago Red Tails!"

Dead. Silence.

More. Dead. Silence.

Even. More. Dead. Silence.

Then she chuckles. "Shut up."

"You think I'm making this up?"

"Who is it?"

"Dex Foster. Google him right fucking now and tell me it's not the same guy."

I hear her putting me on speakerphone and can only assume she's using her phone to look him up. "Ooooh. My. God," she murmurs.

"It's him, isn't it? It's totally him."

"It's very much him. I would recognize those eyes anywhere."

We both say, "Stormy gray" at the same time.

"Holy shit, Tate! I don't...I'm sorry. I don't know what to say. In a roundabout way I feel sort of responsible for all this. I'm the one who encouraged him to hit on you. He looked like your type, you know?"

"He was totally my type." I don't know why my chest hurts so much right now. It's not like Dex and I were a thing. It was one night. Sure, it was one mind-blowing, larger than life, oh-my-God kind of night, but a moment of earth-shattering orgasms doesn't equal soulmates for life or anything.

"I'm really sorry I—"

"No," I stop her. "Please don't apologize for hooking us up because in all seriousness, it was the best night of my life. Ben, err, Dex allowed me to forget about all the difficult things I had gone through up until then. He opened my eyes to what my body deserves and it was hands down the best sex I've ever had. The consequences of our actions are my fault just as much as they are his, I guess."

"What are you going to do?"

"This is where you come in, because I don't know what the fuck to do. Do I tell him? Do I not tell him?"

"If you tell him, you know he'll deny it or throw money at you to walk away."

"That's what I fear will happen as well. I mean, God, for all I know he sleeps with women all the time. He could have fathered more children than Nick Cannon by now."

Eliza giggles. "Doubtful. That man has a serious breeding kink."

"But if I don't tell him, he'll never know he has a kid and his kid will never know their father. How is that fair?"

She's quiet for a minute before she says, "What if you just don't do anything...yet?"

"What do you mean?"

"I mean you're seven months pregnant, Tate. What you don't need is unnecessary stress and although this ordeal seems very necessary, it doesn't have to happen right this moment. You could wait until the baby is born and then decide what to do. Or wait until the season is over even, when you know he'll have more time to dedicate to the situation."

"I don't want him to think I'm trying to trap him into anything. I'm not that person. I'm happy with my life the way it is. I accepted this pregnancy. I've done all the right things to prepare for the baby. I can do this on my own, but also...he deserves to know, right?"

"Okay, if you're asking me, I say wait until the baby is born, snap a picture, and send it to his agent with a note detailing everything. If the baby looks at all like him, he won't be able to deny it's his. If he contacts you, okay. If he doesn't...then we'll know how he feels and what he wants, or, you know, doesn't want."

I nod even though she can't see me. "Yeah. Okay. After the baby comes. That makes sense."

"Tate, you know I'll fly to Chicago and help you in any way I can. I'm totally there when the baby is born, alright? I'll stay with you when your mom and sister have to go back home. We can coordinate so you're not alone until you really feel like you have your feet under you. Especially if you end up with a C-section for any reason. You'll need extra help. Hey, speaking of your mom. What are you doing for Christmas? Will you be in town?"

"No. Doctor doesn't want me to travel this late in the game so my family is coming to me for a couple days."

"All of them?"

"Yep. As far as I know. They rented an Airbnb, so we can all be comfortable for the weekend.

"Aww I bet you're excited to see them."

"Very much." I feel myself smile. "We talk almost daily but it's not the same, you know? Feels like I'm in college all over again and only see them for Christmas break."

"I hear you. I'm glad they're coming down though."

"Yeah. Thank God for a good support system."

"We love you, babe. What's not to love? You're an amazing human who will have an amazing baby and you'll be an amazing mommy."

"Thanks for talking me down, Eliza. I'm glad I got to talk to you tonight."

"Me too. Anytime babe. Call me anytime."

"Love you."

"Love you."

RORY

Still riding with me to the staff xmas party tonight?

ME

Are you sure that's okay? I don't mind driving myself. I can't drink or anything tonight anyway. 😴

RORY

LOL good point, but I won't be drinking tonight either. No way am I getting sloshed if there's even a remote possibility of you going into early labor.

ME

Ummm…you know I'm not due for another six weeks, right?

RORY

Six weeks is nothin' Tate! Shelly had one of her kids eight weeks early. You better have a packed bag in your car just in case.

ME

Oh God! Don't tell me that! You might jinx me into labor! I'll get on that, I promise. Is there parking at your place or should I secure a spot somewhere ahead of time?

RORY

> Oh, there's a parking space underneath my building. You can just follow me to my place and we can change and get ready there.

ME

> Sounds good! See you after dismissal.

RORY

"Wow, you live here?"

After I followed Rory into the city, we park in an underground parking garage that sits beneath a fancy skyrise of luxury condominiums. There's no doubt in my mind this is way above my pay grade and now I wonder just how much money Rory is pulling in as a Kindergarten teacher, or what her lucrative side job must be.

Is she a stripper?

Nah...not Rory.

DoorDash?

I mean maybe...

Personal escort on the weekends?

Professional gambler?

If she's a hooker and this is her pimp's place...

"Yeah. I live with my older brother," she explains, hitting the button to the elevator to take us up to the fifteenth floor."

The top floor?

Isn't that like, a penthouse?

"Is your brother a doctor? A lawyer? Oprah's long-lost brother?"

Rory laughs. "No silly."

"So, what does he do and is he hot, single and does he have a passion for babies in general?

Rory laughs. "If only. You clearly don't know my brother."

"Should I?"

Rory unlocks the door and swings it open. "No. Just seems like everyone in this world does. My brother's a defenseman for the Chicago Red Tails. I can't believe you didn't know that. Have I never told you?"

I feel myself shaking my head but words aren't coming out of my mouth as we step inside her home.

Nooooo.

No, no, no, no.

It can't be.

A spark zips through my chest at the mention of hockey and the Chicago Red Tails, and several thoughts happen all at once.

This isn't happening.

Fuck.

There's no way.

Fuck.

She would've said something.

Fuck.

How did I not know?

Fuuuuuck.

Oh my God...

I swallow the huge knot in my throat and am about to

ask Rory what her brother's name is when the refrigerator door closes and a male voice speaks out.

"Hey Ror, did you put those bottles of wat—" He freezes as we step into the space and his eyes meet mine.

Holy. Fucking. Shit.

It's him.

"It's you," he states with a befuddled stare.

I cannot believe this.

What are the fucking odds?

"Amanda."

"Uhh..." Rory's brow furrows. "Her name is Tate. Tate, this is my brother Dex.

"Dex," I whisper because for some reason I can't get my voice to do more than that.

His brows rise. "Your real name is Tate?"

Continuing to hold Dex's stare, I nod. "Short for Tatum. Everyone calls me Tate."

"Wait." Rory's shoulders fall as she twists between her brother and me, her brows furrowed as she watches us both. "You two know each other? How do you...?" She frowns and swings back to her brother, an angry scorn on her face. "Are you seriously telling me Tate has only been in Chicago since August and you've already found a way to fuck her?"

He holds my gaze but shakes his head. "No."

"Well then how...wait...you called her Amanda." She gasps, her mouth wide open in surprise. "Dex, is this the girl? The one you were hung up on all summer? Amanda Hugginkis?"

Hung up on me?

He's talked about me?

88

He missed me?

When he doesn't answer her, she turns back to me, her eyes bulging. "This can't be happening. Tate, did you vacation in Key West this summer?"

Slowly, I nod, still refusing to take my eyes off the man who has invaded my every dream since the day I left. His square jaw clenches and his eyes fall over the rest of my body and suddenly I feel naked in front of him once again, only this time, much more vulnerable as I now have an unmistakable baby bump I can't even pretend to hide.

"And you hooked up with my brother on vacation?" Rory's unending line of questions brings me back to my senses. She gasps and her eyes bulge even more. "Oh, my God, Tatum! Is my brother your baby daddy?"

"Whoa. What?"

Her words are like a record coming to a screeching halt. *Fuck.*

I squeeze my eyes closed. My heart tumbles down through my stomach.

"What the fuck did you just say?" Dex lowers his water bottle to the counter, bracing it with his two hands. He gazes at me again, eyes falling to my very pregnant baby belly, and then bulges his eyes at his sister. "Rory Jean Foster is Tatum...*the* friend?"

"What?"

His words come out flustered and fast. "The one you were...you know. The one you were telling me about when the school year started. The new teacher friend with the... you know, the..." He makes a rounded gesture over his stomach.

"Oh, my God, Rory, you told your brother I was pregnant?"

She flips her head between the two of us. "I...you texted me that day and I was here and..." She gestures to me. "It's kind of blatantly obvious now, don't you think?"

"You're pregnant." Dex stares.

"Looks that way, doesn't it?" Sorry not sorry for my unfiltered sass.

He shakes his head, his forehead wrinkled. "Wait...and you think—"

"It has to—

"Rory!" Dex shouts.

"Alright! Alright! YES!" She flails her arms, her tote bag still in hand. "Dex, meet Tate, one of Riverside's new first grade teachers, though I'm pretty sure you not only know her already, you probably know her better than I do at this point." She turns to me. "And Tate, meet Dex, my brother, and the man who I guess gave you the best fuck of your life according to you, though I wish I didn't know that, and seemingly knocked you up at the same time. There. I said it. Now it's out in the open. Can we be adults about this now?"

"What the fuck are you playing at?" Dex's words are now targeted at me.

"Me? What are you—"

"How did you even find me?"

"Wait." I shake my head. "What?"

"Please tell me you are not that psycho to have conjured up this grand scheme?

"Come again?" I rear back, not understanding what he's trying to say.

"What, did you figure out who I was when you left Florida, and now you're here to try and trap me in some..." His face contorts to one of disgust. "Fucking parent trap?"

"Dex," Rory tries to stop him, but he only has eyes for me at the moment, and to my misfortune, they're anything but loving.

"No." I shake my head. My eyes fill with unshed tears. This is not a situation I ever thought I would find myself in, but exactly what I feared would happen. "I didn't know y—"

"You're really here right now? We haven't seen each other or talked to each other since that night because you left me without a trace, and now you're here to tell me you're pregnant and you think I'm the father?"

"Dex I..." I shake my head. "There hasn't been anyone else. Not since..."

"I wore a condom sweetheart," he says, shaking his head with disdain. "I *always* wear a condom."

Rory scoffs, mumbling, "Not always fool proof."

"Shut it, Rory."

"No. You need to quit being an asshole before y—"

"It's okay," I stop them both, finally finding my brave button. Rory and Dex both turn toward me. "It's fine. I can do this by myself. I didn't come here to spring this on anybody. I only just found out who you were a few days ago when I saw you on TV." I hold my hands up in defense. "I didn't know you played hockey and I didn't know you were related to Rory. I'm sorry. I am. Rory, for putting you in this awkward position and Dex for...well, I guess for all of it. You gave me the best night of my life and now I'm dealing with the consequences of our actions."

Finally, my tears spill over and down my cheeks. My body is trembling because I hate confrontation, but if there's one thing I've learned over the past year, it's that nobody sticks up for me in this world but me. I'm all I have. All I can trust.

"But I will not let you stand here and tell me this is all my fault," I continue. "I didn't ask for this. I moved away from an asshole once. I certainly don't plan to get involved with another one. And if you think for one second I did this on purpose t-t-to trap you or take your money..." I huff. "Then you don't know me at all."

Rory sighs, her head tilting. "Tate,"

"I should go."

"No," Dex says. His mesmerizing eyes the color of storm clouds carrying considerable pain and abounding confusion gaze at me as he steps forward only to shove past me to the front door. "Don't bother. I'm out of here."

"Dex!"

"I can't Rory!"

And that's all he says before he slams the door.

The moment he leaves, I release the sob I was holding back. Rory wraps her hand softly around my arm. "I promise he'll come around."

Even if he does, do I want him to?

I can't raise my baby with an asshole father.

And right now, that's what Dex Foster is. An asshole.

I might be scared out of my mind, but I'll be damned if I put myself and my child in a loveless, unhappy living situation.

I won't do it.

9
DEX

"FuuuuuUUUUUCK!" I shout once I'm in the privacy of my truck. I rest my elbows on my steering wheel and my head in my hands, reminding myself to take a few deep breaths.

"What the fuck just happened?"

I've done nothing but think about her for months and there she was, standing in my fucking living room.

And then suddenly, I'm about to be a dad?

No fucking way.

Not happening.

There's no way that kid is mine.

"There hasn't been anyone else..."

Is she the type of person to lie about something like this?

She didn't seem that way all those months ago.

Honestly, she looked scared tonight.

Ugh! Fuck!

Tapping my phone a few times, I send a text to the team's group chat.

ME

Malone, I'm picking you up in ten. Nelson, we're coming to you.

HAWK

Uh. Okay...everything okay?

ME

No. I'll explain when we get there.

MILO

What's going on?

COLBY

Guess I'll put some clothes on.

ZEKE

Can't be there. Elsie is napping. Sorry man. Call me if you need me.

QUINTON

Oooh, Dexter gossip? I'm on my way!

My tires screech as I turn out of the parking garage and then step on the gas to reach Hawken before I seriously flip my shit. My mind is racing and I can't calm it down. No amount of knitting is going to make this go away and I don't know what to do.

Hawk lives in a smaller condo just about ten blocks from me so I'm in front of his building in under eight minutes, but he's ready for me. He steps out of the lobby, thanking the doorman, and hops into my truck and we're off to Colby's.

"Foster," he says, turning to look at my face. "What's up, bro?"

"I think I'm completely fucked. That's what's up." I

clench my jaw, frustrated with myself for the way I handled the entire last fifteen minutes of my life.

"How was I supposed to handle it though?" I ask myself much to Hawk's confusion.

"Handle what? Dude, what's going on? And watch your speed. You don't need to be on the front page for a fuckin' speeding violation."

"Fuck it. I'll offer the cop season tickets."

Malone scoffs. "Yeah, because that's legal."

I huff a few times trying to decide how I want to talk about this but Hawken is my best friend on the team. He's like a brother to me. I mean they all are, but Hawken is the one I'm closest to. He gets my humor. He gets my craziness and he doesn't judge me for it. "I don't know if I fucked up or if I'm being fucked, man. And it's driving me crazy."

"Alright," he drawls. "You want to fill in some gaps for me?"

"The girl. Remember the girl? My girl, from Key West?"

He grins. "Amanda Hugginkis."

Fuck, hearing hear name makes my dick twitch and sends a sharp pain through my chest at the same time.

"Yeah. Her name is Tatum. She's here."

"She's here?"

"She's in town."

"You saw her?"

"Yeah. In my house. Standing in my living room."

He shakes his head, his eyes narrowing. "I don't—"

"With my sister!"

"Rory?"

"I only have one sister, man. You know that."

"Tatum is in town and she's hanging out with Rory?"

"Yeah."

"How did that happen?"

"Supposedly she's a new teacher at Rory's elementary school or some shit."

He's quiet for a second and then purses his lips. "Sooooo why are you here with me in your truck and not fucking her brains out right now? Isn't she what you were pining for all fucking summer?"

"Yeah. She is...was....is...ugh fuck. I don't know."

"What do you mean you don't know? Dex, you've done nothing but talk about how much you lo—"

"She's pregnant, Hawk." There. I said it.

I blow out a slightly stuttered breath.

"Pregnant?"

"That's what I said. Very pregnant in fact."

"Ooookay."

"And she says it's mine."

He scoffs. "And you believe her?"

"That's just the thing...I didn't believe her. I basically told her to go fuck herself and left."

"Oh shit."

"Yeah."

We pull into Colby's driveway just as Milo and Charlee do. They can both sense the tension when I step out of my truck but Charlee is the first one to me, wrapping me up in a hug like she's been known to do.

"Whatever it is, Dex, we're here for you."

My tension softens a bit as it does every time Charlee's around. Not because of some weird crush I have or anything like that. I respect her a lot for the things she's gone through and whenever she's around I try hard to rein in my temper so she never has to feel the anger and contempt she had to put up with when she was with her asshole of an ex. None of us on the team ever want to put her back in that headspace so we all try to calm our emotions when she's around.

I suspect that's exactly why Milo brought her along.

He knows if I'm pissed, it's bad.

"Thanks Charlee. I promise I'll be good. It's just been a crazy fucked up last hour of my life."

"Anything I can do?"

"I wish, but also, I doubt it."

Together, we make our way into Colby and Carissa's house, the entire group standing around the kitchen watching Carissa and Charlee prepare snacks for us because it's what we do when we're together. When we're not playing hockey or talking about hockey, we're eating.

I give everyone the basic run down as I did for Malone on the way here and for the most part, everyone remains silent until I get all the words out. And when I tell them how I left things with Tatum, Carissa and Charlee share a glance.

"What? What did that mean?" I gesture between the two of them. "Why did you just look at her like that? Spill it, Smallson."

Carissa's cringe says enough, but I heed her words anyway as the punishment I'm pretty sure I deserve.

"Dex, I think you fucked up. And I say that with all the love in the world."

Charlee nods. "Agreed."

"Fuck." I push my hand through my hair. "What the hell do I do?"

"Did you not use protection, bro?" Quinton asks me. "I know you took some with you."

"Fuck yeah, I used a damn condom. I don't go anywhere without them. You know that."

"Yeah, but how hard were you fuckin'?"

I'm about to answer 'pretty damn hard' but Carissa waves off the question.

"Doesn't matter. The end result is the same. You slept with her and now she's pregnant."

"Exactly. You have to put yourself in her shoes," Charlee explains. "Though I know that's much easier said than done. Let's say it is yours."

I relent with a sigh. "Okay."

"If everything she's ever told you is true and she's newly divorced, moving to a new town with a new job and finding out she's pregnant, that's more than enough to probably have her scared out of her ever-loving mind."

"Right." Carissa nods in a tag-team explanation. "But then to add fuel to the fire, she finds out who you are and that you're living in the same town as she is and she only barely gets the chance to react to that before you're finding out she's pregnant."

"And before either one of you can talk rationally about it, you're telling her she's full of shit and accusing her of trying to trap you into a relationship." Charlee finishes.

With each passing sentence, I cringe harder and harder. "Fuck, you guys. You're making it sound like I'm the world's biggest dick."

They don't respond in words. Only a shrug and a slight eyebrow raise.

That's loud enough.

I get it.

I blow out a resigned sigh. "Because I was a dick."

With his arms crossed over his chest and leaning against the kitchen cabinets, Colby asks, "Do you have any reason to think she's lying to you?"

"No. I don't, but what if she is lying? What if for some Godforsaken reason this is all a scam? What if she slept with someone else in the last however many months?"

"You can demand a paternity test. Get lawyers involved."

"If she's not lying, she'll hate you for that," Carissa scolds her husband. "Just sayin'."

I scoff at her. "For trying to protect myself?"

"Did she try to contact you in any way up until earlier today?"

"No."

"And how pregnant is she?" She counts back to May. "She would have to be what...seven or eight months or so?"

"Sure. Yeah. I don't know."

"Dex, that's pretty damn pregnant. Do the math here. A little over seven months ago we were in Key West. If she was trying to trap you, she wouldn't have waited seven months to do it."

Finally, I lift my head, staring back at Carissa, defeated. "You think so?"

"I feel ninety-nine percent certain. She would've either been taking pregnancy tests like three weeks out and would've contacted your agent or she would wait to have the baby and then tell the world it's yours so you would send her money to shut her up."

A pit of unease grows in my stomach and for the first time since I can remember, I feel like I need to vomit. Tatum was nothing but an amazing human when we were together in Key West and she's all I've thought about since that magical night. The moment I saw her in my living room I wanted to pick her up and crash my lips to hers and never let her go, but something was different about her this time. Other than the obvious change to her physique.

Maybe it was fear?

Maybe it was shock?

Maybe she really didn't know I lived there.

"Fuck. I messed up."

Milo claps my shoulder. "But there's never been a fuck up you couldn't fix, Dex."

"I can't fix pregnant, Milo."

"Nope. You can't. But if that baby is yours..."

"I know."

If the baby really is mine, I'll step up and do the right thing. Whatever that is.

"You know there's one person you can call who might be able to give you a little peace of mind," Colby suggests.

As if.

"Oh yeah? And who's that?"

"Elias. Or if you want a female perspective...Whitney." He shrugs like calling his brother and sister-in-law is a no-brainer. "They had a one-night stand at our wedding in New Orleans. I had no idea he actually knew her, and I guess thank God he did or else he may never have been given the opportunity to be that little one's dad. Things have worked out well for them. I'm sure they would sit down and talk this through with you."

"I suppose that's not a terrible idea."

"How do you feel about all this?" Colby finally asks now that I'm calm.

Worried.

Scared out of my ever loving mind.

Confused.

Overwhelmed.

Irritated.

Defeated.

"I don't know how I feel right now. I think I—"

"Where the fuck is he?" The front door slams as my sister's voice pierces through the foyer.

I lower my head. "Oh shit."

Rory makes her grand entrance into the kitchen and punches me as hard as she can on my upper arm. "What the fuck is wrong with you?"

"Ow!" I grab my arm. When she goes to try it again, Hawk wraps an arm around her, effectively caging her in.

"That's enough Ror."

"Enough? This douche nozzle doesn't know what enough is. He only ever thinks with his dick regardless of the goddamn consequences, isn't that right, DICKSTER?"

I cringe at the new nickname, apropos as it may be.

"You stupid fucking asshole!" Rory rages. "How could you do that to her?"

"Rory, I didn't mean t—"

"You should've seen her after you stormed out! A sobbing mess and scared out of her damn mind. Do you have any idea what she's going through right now?"

I have a small idea, yeah.

"I—"

"She has nobody, Dex. NOBODY! She's less than six weeks away from giving birth and you just stomped all over her and made her feel like a lying sack of shit."

"I know, Rory!" I shout back. "Fuck. I know, alright?"

Still wrapped in Hawk's arms, she points at me with a tight glare. "You better fucking fix this, brother.

"I will."

"How exactly?"

I toss my head back, growling in frustration. "I don't know. I wasn't exactly prepared for this."

"Yeah, well, neither was Tatum."

She holds my stare until I'm so uncomfortable I have to look away. "I'll talk to Tatum. She deserves an apology."

"Damn right, she does."

"Easy there, Foster," Hawk murmurs in her ear.

The tension isn't leaving my body though, no matter how calm Rory is or how quiet everyone around us is. My head is nothing but a raging storm of fear and anxiety and worry.

Pushing both hands through my hair, I look around the room and finally say what's been on my mind since I hopped in my truck and peeled out of the parking garage.

"I don't know how to be a good dad."

Fucking tears spring to my eyes and I can feel my chin quiver.

God, I feel like such a pussy.

I lock eyes with my sister again and say to her, "Our sperm donor was a piece of shit. He did nothing for us. We barely knew who he was."

Rory doesn't respond, but I see the unshed tears in her eyes.

"How am I supposed to be the person she needs? I don't know what the fuck I'm doing! All I know is how to defend the puck. I can play hockey. That's it."

"Bullshit." Quinton shakes his head. "You know a lot more than that, man. Give yourself a little more credit."

Milo clears his throat. "I don't have any children, Dex, but I imagine she doesn't need a magician right now. And she doesn't need someone with all the right answers. She just needs someone she can count on to support her."

"She doesn't want your fucking money, Dex," Rory announces.

"I didn't mean financially." Milo shakes his head. "Though if it were me, she wouldn't pay a dime if I could more than afford it. I mean she needs someone she can depend on to hold her hand through the next several months. No doubt she's scared. You're scared. So be scared together so it's not as bad for either of you."

"Landric's right." Colby nods. "We've all rallied around Zeke, haven't we? Elsie is the most loved little kid in Chicago when any of us are around her. If you think for even a minute we're going to let you fail..."

"Not to mention you've literally been talking about Tatum since the day we left Florida and she's right here. In your town and carrying your child." Charlee beams. "If that's not fate, I don't know what is."

"What if she hates me? What if nothing between us is right?"

"Do you honestly believe that?"

No.

"Everything about her felt so right when we were together. I would've done anything for her. I would've given her the world. I would've asked her to stay if I hadn't fallen asleep. That's my biggest regret."

Carissa rubs my arm and wraps hers around me. "I think once you talk to her, you'll find things are going to work out just fine. Try not to overreact. Your feelings are very valid, but remember, you're not the only one feeling them. Just be there for her. That's all she needs."

My eyes flit to my sister who is wiping tears from her cheeks. She nods to me, agreeing with the ladies trying to help pull my shit together.

Somewhere inside me, I find the strength to pick my head up and take a deep breath. Steeling myself to take the first step forward, I turn to Rory.

"Where can I find Tatum?"

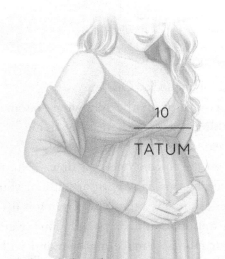

10

TATUM

Knock, knock, knock.

My brow furrows at the knock on my door. With my sister still on the phone I walk to the door and look through the peep hole.

Oh God.

It's him.

"Uh, Tessa, I gotta go. I'll call you back, alright?"

"Yeah. Everything good?"

"Uh yeah. Delivery guy."

"Oooooh gotcha. Talk later. Bye Sis."

"Bye."

I lay my phone on the counter and step to the door, opening it wide to find a breathtakingly gorgeous man, albeit a melancholy one, standing on the other side. A white paper bag in hand that I could smell before I even opened the door.

Mmm Chinese.

"Hey," he says softly.

"Hey."

"Can I come in?"

"That depends."

He rubs the back of his neck. "On?"

"On whether or not any of the following statements answers any of the things you came here to say to me."

"Alright."

I tick them off on my fingers one at a time. "Number one. Clearly, I'm keeping this baby with or without you so do not even consider asking me otherwise. Giving it up for adoption is not an option. Number two, I don't want a fucking dime of your money. I make my own and will be just fine without you. Number three, I'm not moving away nor am I ignoring your sister and if you can't live with that then fuck you very much and be on your way."

He continues to stand in my doorway, one hand in his pocket. His steel gray eyes penetrate me as if he can see right through me. Right through my confidence and determination until he's staring into my frightened, anxious, and emotional reality.

But he's not moving.

"You're still here."

Without a change to his facial expression, he gestures inside with his chin. "Can I come in?"

Without verbally responding, I move aside and allow him to step into my apartment, closing the door behind him and turning to watch him as he looks around my place. I'm aware this apartment is laughable compared to the penthouse palace he lives in, but it's clean, and it's what I can afford on my own so close to the city and I won't feel bad for that. As he glances around, I'm able to get a good look at the father of my child for the first time. A man I've only ever seen through lust-filled lenses.

He's tall. Well, taller than my five foot five inches. He has at least a foot on me. He's wearing a pair of jeans that show off his powerful legs and a black long-sleeved shirt that hugs his tight arms and hides the most beautifully sculpted chest I've ever seen. His hair is cleanly buzzed around the sides but messy on top. Enough to run his fingers through, which he's done once or twice since he walked in. His stubbled square jaw clenches and he fidgets with the bag in his hand. I can tell he's nervous, though he hasn't said anything.

So, I guess I'm the captain of this ship now.

Rip off the Band-Aid.

"Why are you here, Dex?"

He turns and his sad eyes meet mine, making me feel all kinds of ways. Part of me is longing for him to wrap his arms around me and tell me how much he's thought about me. How much he's missed me so I can say the same and we can replay that night in Key West. I might be seven months pregnant but I'm horny as hell these days. But the practical part of me knows I can't get involved with someone who so easily dismissed me without even giving us a chance to talk first.

"I think I owe you a big apology, Tatum."

Well, that's not at all what I expected him to say.

"You *think* you do?"

He sighs. "I know I do. Look, I'm not good at this, alright? And I don't really know what to say other than I'm sorry." When he raises his arms, he realizes he's still holding onto a paper bag. "Oh, and I brought egg rolls

SUSAN RENEE

from Wong's. It's the best Chinese in town and...well, Rory told me you've been craving egg rolls so...you know." He offers me the bag and I hesitantly take it from him.

I'm drooling already.

"That's very sweet of you. Thank you." To hide my blush, I retreat to the kitchen. "Can I get you a drink?"

"Uh, sure. Yeah. What have you got?"

I open the fridge and call out, "Orange juice, milk, water...Tequila."

"A tequila screwdriver sounds great. That'll work."

I huff a soft chuckle to myself as I pour his requested drink, and then pour a straight OJ for myself.

"What's so funny?" He's watching me from the doorway of my kitchen, arms folded across his chest.

"You are. I didn't take you for a fruity cocktail kind of guy."

"Well, you didn't offer whiskey or bourbon and I didn't think asking for straight tequila would be a good idea, but alcohol is good for the nerves."

"You're nervous?"

"As fuck. You can't tell?"

The corner of my lip stretches in a quick smile. "Maybe a little."

I expect to see him smirking back at me but all I see when I glance his way is pain and fear in his eyes.

"Tatum, I'm really sorry for earlier. I..." He pushes his hand through his hair. "I don't know what came over me. I was an absolute dick, but that's not who I am and I need you to know that."

I step past him into my living room and curl onto the

108

couch, my left leg tucked under me. He follows and sits opposite me, his sheer size taking up most of the couch.

"Shit. I forgot the egg rolls."

I move to get up but he places a hand on my leg and jumps up. "I got it. You stay."

Dex grabs the bag and hunts through my kitchen cabinets until he finds my plates, snagging two and bringing them along. He hands me a plate and I serve myself an egg roll, taking a bite out of it the moment it's in my hand.

"MmmmGod, this is good," I moan, letting my head fall back as I savor the taste I've been craving for days. "Thank you, Dex."

He clears his throat and shifts in his seat watching me, his pupils slightly dilated and a lighter shade of gray than before. "You're welcome."

I take a minute to chew my food and then tell him what I wish I could've told him a few hours ago.

"I'm sorry for all this too. Had I known you lived in this area, I..." the heat in my cheeks returns and I hate that he can probably see it. "Who am I kidding? As soon as I found out who you were I knew I wouldn't contact you. Not now anyway."

"Why?"

"Several reasons. For starters, I didn't want to bother you."

"Bother me? What do you mean?"

I cock my head. "Come on, Dex. Look at you and look at me."

"I'm looking..."

"You're this celebrity hockey player and you live in a penthouse palace. I teach first grade and I live...well, here."

I throw out my arm and gesture around us. "We clearly come from two different worlds."

His brows pinch and his lips separate as if he's about to say something but I don't give him the chance.

"But listen, I swear to God, I didn't know I was pregnant right away and then when I found out, I had no idea who you were. I knew your name wasn't Ben Dover so I had no way of trying to find you."

"You really didn't recognize me in Key West?"

"Uh, no. I'm sorry. It's not that I never follow hockey, but it was always more my brothers' thing. A few Detroit players' names might ring a bell if I heard them, but other than that..." I shake my head. "That's about as far as my hockey fandom goes."

His shoulders fall a bit and I honestly can't tell if he's disappointed or relieved at my confession. His eyes fall to my stomach.

"And you're certain it's mine?"

I bow my head, closing my eyes and taking a reassuring breath because what I'm about to say to him might blow his mind.

"Dex, I've only ever had sex with one man in my entire life until the night I met you. And there's been nobody since you, but if you want me to get a patern—"

"Are you shitting me right now?" His jaw drops.

I shake my head.

"Dear...God." His hands are back in his hair and he stands up from the couch, pacing in my living room. "How old are you, Tatum?"

"Thirty-one. Why?"

He clasps his chest and releases his breath. "Oh, thank fuck."

"How old did you think I was?"

"Doesn't matter," he tells me, his eyes wide. "I just needed to know you're legal because fuck, Tatum, we...and then we did that...God it was so...shit. I didn't mean to hurt you that night and if I did, I'm sorry." He gestures to my body. "And now this. Fuck! You must think I'm some kind of monster!"

"What? No! Why would I think that?"

"Why *would* you..." He shakes his head. "Tatum, you've only ever slept with one man your whole life and then you gave yourself to me, the hornball hockey player who came on to you on vacation. And don't get me started on all the shit we—"

"I liked it, Dex."

He stops. "What?"

"I'm a grown ass woman who very much enjoyed every minute we spent together, so calm your tits for one damn second and sit down. You're making me anxious."

Baffled by my sudden burst in attitude he does what I ask of him but he keeps his head bowed. "I'm sorry."

"Don't be. I loved that night with you, Dex, so if you're over there thinking you took advantage of me, you can wipe that thought right out of your mind because if anybody took advantage of anybody, it was the other way around."

His glassy eyes pierce mine but he remains speechless.

"I wanted you, Dex. I was lonely and I wanted someone to make me feel good and there you were offering yourself to me and so I took the chance and I have zero regrets."

His eyes fall to my stomach. "None?"

"Not one. You gave me back to myself that night, Dex. Not once in my six years of marriage to Michael, did he ever treat me the way you did. He never touched me the way you did. Never spoke to me the way you did. You showed me what I'm worthy of. What I'm capable of. What I deserve. And I'm grateful for that. It was hands down the best sex of my life and I haven't forgotten it. Not one minute of one day."

He still doesn't say anything but at least now he's looking at me. Watching me.

"And so, I got pregnant." I shrug. "We could spend all night talking about the should-a, could-a, would-a, but it won't change anything. I'm growing a human inside of me and that's something I had to come to terms with. And I have. I'm perfectly capable of raising this baby on my own. My intention wasn't to steamroll you with this information. You are under no obligation to do anything here. I'm not asking you for a thing."

"I want to do something."

"O-Okay."

"I can't just let you go through this alone, Tatum."

"It's not like I haven't gone through the last seven months—"

"I know. And I feel terrible about that. I'm not a totally immoral man, Tatum. It might take me a hot minute to wrap my head around this whole situation, but I want to do the right thing. I want to be here for the baby. And for you."

"Dex, you can be as involved or as uninvolved as you want. I know your hockey comes first. Your schedule is going to be busy. I get th—"

"I'm all in, Tatum." He turns his body to face me, his warm hand sliding over mine. "One hundred and ten percent. I'm in. I want to be in."

I tilt my head noting the sincerity in his voice and in his eyes. "You're sure? Please don't feel like you have to do th—"

"I want to." He squeezes my hand. "Look, I know the season is going to take me away and I'm going to hate it when I have to miss something. I already feel extremely guilty that you've had to do so much on your own, so please, let me do this with you. Whatever you need. I want to be there. I'll be there. And you're not paying a dime."

I cock my head, ready for a fight, but he stops me. "I'm sorry, Tatum, but I can't agree to all your terms. I need you to give me this one."

My shoulders fall. "Dex."

"No." He shakes his head. "Sorry. This is the one time I'm going to pull salary rank. I can more than afford your prenatal care, Tatum. Please allow me to take care of whatever is left. If you have medical bills from past visits, I'll pay them. Please. I promise I won't overstep. This is the very least I can do. Please let me take this responsibility."

"You know you can't just throw money at this and make it go away?"

"I promise you, that's not what I'm trying to do, but you and I both know I make a shit ton more money than you do. And I don't want this to go away. I mean, that's not to say I'm not sorry for putting you in this predicament in the first place. Knocking you up certainly wasn't my intention, but you're here now and I don't want you to go. I'm glad you're here. I want you here, Tatum. I...I want this baby." He sighs. "I don't know what I'm doing, but I'll figure it out with your help. I want our baby." He squeezes my hand once more. "So, save your money. Save it for...whatever. Get pedicures every day or treat yourself to whatever you want, just let me do this one thing. I can't carry this baby for you but I can damn well pay for whatever you both need. Please let me spend my money on something good."

I'm not sure what to say to him. This feels like I'm just using him for his money and I hate that feeling, but he seems sincere in his words. I would like to think if he was as upset about this pregnancy news as he was a couple hours ago, he wouldn't be here. He wouldn't be offering anything.

He would be trying to get rid of me.

But he's not.

He's here.

Whatever that means for us.

He's here.

"Alright." I nod. "Thank you, Dex."

He brings my hands to his lips and kisses the back of each one. "Thank *you*, Tatum."

"Can I ask you something?"

"Anything."

"How are really feeling about all this?" He's pensive for a moment and then gives me the faintest of smiles.

"I would be lying if I said I wasn't scared out of my fucking mind."

"Is that all?"

He huffs a quiet laugh. "Besides being pissed at myself for being a dick to you earlier? Yeah. Scared. Nervous. Anxious. Whatever synonym you've got for scared. That's how I'm feeling." His gaze slips from mine and he swallows hard. "I don't know how to be a good dad, Tatum."

My heart flips in my chest at his confession and tears well in my eyes.

"I didn't have the best role model growing up." He leans forward, resting his elbows on his knees. "I just don't want to mess this up. I don't want to be a failure."

"I had wonderful parents growing up. I still have wonderful parents, but that doesn't make me any less scared of completely failing this kid." I take his hand in mine. "Maybe it's a new parent thing, I don't know. But it's a little nicer knowing I'm not alone."

"I'm sorry in advance, okay? In case I do something stupid or I lose my balance and stumble along the way. I'm sorry, Tatum, but I'm going to try. I'll try like hell."

"We'll get through this together."

He nods quietly, thinking to himself before he nervously glances at me and asks, "Do you think I could get your number?"

Seeing puppy dog eyes on a big man like Dex makes me laugh. His personality is a one-hundred-and-eighty-degree change from the man I met in Key West. But I like this man. Confident when he wants to be, and humble enough to allow himself to be vulnerable. "Yes, I think that can be arranged."

"So, it went well, then?" Milo asks while changing his clothes after our morning session. The team was back on the ice, running drills and preparing for our next string of away games. Though we see each other during the summer, there's nothing like the camaraderie we have during the season. These guys are my brothers. My family. I don't know what I would do without them.

"I guess as well as could be expected." I shrug. "She listened. She accepted my apology and she definitely wasn't about to take any of my shit."

Colby pulls a clean t-shirt over his shoulders. "She's going to let you be involved?"

"She's not letting me. I want to be. I promised her I would give one hundred and ten percent whenever I'm here. It just sucks that I'll miss things when I'm away. And it's killing me that she's done everything these last few months on her own. Had I known, I would've been there. I could've helped her."

"I mean, sure you could run to the store for her or give her a foot rub when she needs it." Zeke shrugs. "But you can't carry that baby for her. You can't endure whatever uncomfortableness she's going through. You do what you can when you can. I won't say it doesn't suck when you're away because it fucking does. Your life will change though and you won't even know it. You won't want to be hanging at Pringle's after a game when you can be snuggled in a chair holding your kid feeling them breathe peacefully on your chest while they fall asleep. Stuff like that...it's the best feeling in the world."

"But what if I pat its back too hard or, I don't know, squeeze too hard when I'm holding it? How do I not break my kid?"

The guys laugh around me and Zeke nods. "Dude, I had those same fears, but I promise you when you're holding your kid in your arms, everything about you changes. You'll do anything to protect that child. Give them the moon when they ask for it. You won't break it. I promise."

"Yeah. I don't know what the hell I'm doing, but I'll be damned if I fail this kid. And to be honest, I don't want to fail Tatum either. I downloaded this baby app so I can keep up with where she is in the process and what she might be going through. I'm trying to learn all I can as quickly as possible."

"Speaking of Tatum, what's the deal with you two now?" Quinton asks. "Are you officially together?"

"Uh, I guess I never really considered that, nor did we talk about it last night." I scratch my head, slightly irritated I didn't think to bring it up. "I don't really know what we are at the moment. Do you think that's what she wants?"

Milo steps into his shoe and bends over to tie the laces. "What would you want if you had your way?"

I haven't given it much thought either.

That's bullshit.

She's all I've thought about for months and now she's here, living in Chicago and carrying my child

If Tatum told me she would be okay with whatever I wanted, what would I want? I've never given thought to having a relationship with someone because I didn't think I could be a good partner to anyone. Sexual partner, sure, but the lovey-dovey stuff? The caring and the spending time and the affection...

That was never me.

It wasn't me growing up.

It's not me now.

But when I saw Tatum standing in my living room, my world flipped upside down. My heart raced and my body burned for her. Everything about our night in Florida rushed back and I could've happily replayed every moment with her. And then this whole baby thing smacked me in the face and everything changed.

I was scared.

I was angry.

I was confused.

I was overwhelmed.

I was in denial.

I'm still a lot of those things, but when push comes to shove, I'm attracted to Tatum, and not just in a sexual way. Yes, her body is a man's wonderland, there's no denying that. She's even more beautiful to me knowing it's my child she's carrying inside her. But there's so much more I want to know about her. I want to know all about her. Every detail she's willing to share.

"I think if I had my way, I would entertain the idea of being with her. Maybe." I shake my head. "I don't know. Maybe I'm stupid for thinking that. I knocked her up and then she disappeared from my life. She can't possibly be interested."

Colby caps my shoulder. "You're not stupid for having those thoughts at all, man. I think you're pretty normal. You clearly like her. She's all you've talked about for months. Don't push that away because of what you think you might know but really have no idea."

Christmas sucked.

I wasn't able to see Tatum while she was with her family, nor did she think it was a good idea to introduce me just yet. Given my popularity and umm, reputation for playing the field, she didn't want to put a damper on anyone's holiday. I guess I understand but I wish I could've told her family that I'm in this one hundred percent. I wish I could've looked her father in the eye and told him I plan to be there every step of the way from here on out with his daughter.

Hopefully I'll get that chance in the near future. Before the baby comes.

Once her time with family was over, Tatum did something for me I never expected her to do and I'm pretty damn sure it's going to completely rock my world. Though we're only days away from the end of the year, she secured an extra ultrasound with her doctor so I could see the baby she's been watching grow inside her for the last seven months. I don't even care that her insurance doesn't cover it. I'm more than ecstatic to pay for it. When she told me she made the appointment and asked if I would be available, I almost fucking cried.

After all this time, she went and did something nice like this for me?

Hell yes, I want to see our baby.

But at the same time, I am nervous as fucking hell.

Everything becomes very real today. Real for me.

We should be at about thirty weeks by now and from the app I downloaded online our baby should be roughly the size of a pineapple and should weigh about two and a half to three pounds.

A pineapple.

Tatum has a pineapple inside her that has my DNA.

The thought absolutely blows my mind.

"You know I could've taken the L into town and met you," she says when she answers her door.

"Like I would ever make you take the train. Do you know how many germs are on that thing?"

She juts her hip out, her hand on her side. "Do you know how many germ-infested children I spend eight hours a day with five days a week?"

She has a point.

"Fair." I shrug. "But then I wouldn't have been able to bring you these." She smiles when I hand her the bouquet of yellow and pink roses. "Uh, I wanted to get you tropical ones like we would've seen in Key West but it's wintertime in Chicago sooo they're not exactly in season, I guess. The colors were bright though and they reminded me of you so..."

"Thank you, Dex. They're beautiful. Let me put them in water quickly before we go."

"Are you okay?"

"Hmm?" she asks from the kitchen where I follow her, watching her from the doorway.

"Something's wrong. What's wrong? Are you not feeling well? We can reschedule the—"

"No." She shakes her head. "I'm fine."

I narrow my eyes further, studying her mannerisms. She's not walking like she's in pain, but she's also not as animated as I've seen her before and that makes me nervous. When I don't budge from the doorway, she sets her vase down on the counter and finally makes eye contact.

"I'm just nervous. That's all."

"What are you nervous about? Is there something to be nervous about?"

"No. Not at all. Everything is fine. It's just a thing with me, I think, but every time I go in for an ultrasound my fears get the best of me and I'm scared there will be something wrong with the baby."

I'm away from the doorway in an instant, wrapping my arms around her whether she wants me to or not. The need to let her know she's not alone overpowering any other train of thought. "How many ultrasounds have you had?"

"Uh...three? Four maybe?"

"And everything has been fine every time?"

"Yeah. There was just this one time about two months ago that the baby wasn't moving much and it freaked me out and I ended up in the doctor's office sobbing that something was wrong and baby was just asleep." She shakes her head, embarrassed.

"The doctor did a quick ultrasound and assured me everything was okay, but that doesn't change the fact that something can always go wrong. No pregnancy is guaranteed. My mother had several miscarriages between my siblings and me. Pregnancy complications come up all the time. It's always a possibility."

I can feel her tension in my arms and I ache to make it better for her. A pang of guilt shoots through me that I never considered the fear and trepidation Tatum must be experiencing on a regular basis and that she's had to do it all alone. New mothers maneuver through more ups and downs during a pregnancy than those of us without a uterus can possibly comprehend. Sharing their bodies to bring life into this world is scary shit. I should've known she might be nervous. I'm nervous and I'm not half the superhero she is.

Releasing her body, I tip her chin with my finger. "Hey. Look at me."

Her ocean blue eyes meet mine. "Everything is going to be fine. I'll be right by your side and I promise I won't leave you, alright? I'm sorry I haven't been here. I'm sorry I've missed so damn much, but I'm here now. We'll cross the rest of these bridges together, wherever they lead us."

She swallows and gives me a tiny nod and without hesitating, I lean forward and plant a kiss to her forehead. "I'm sorry I wasn't thinking. It never dawned on me you might be nervous." I smooth my hands down her arms. "But thank you for telling me. I want to know these things, okay? I want to be here for you."

"Thank you, Dex."

Trying to change the subject to something a little happier, I open the front door and ask, "So, do you know if it's a boy? Or a girl?"

She chuckles softly and rubs her hand down her belly. "Nah, I decided I didn't want to know unless I happened to see a blatantly obvious ultrasound. So far, when I'm looking at the screen, the baby has not been in a position for me to see. And besides, I don't care what it is as long as it's healthy."

That stops me in my tracks as we head out the door. "Wait. You don't want to find out what we're having?"

"Why would I?"

"Because...uh...like, don't we need to plan shit? Like pink or blue and what about names? What about nursery plans." My brow furrows. "Where are you going to put that, by the way?"

Does she even have room for that here?

Maybe we should be looking for a new place.

A place for all of us?

Would she want that?

Should we live together even if we're not together-together?

Tatum laughs. "Dex, I'm a month and a half from pushing this thing out of my vagina. There's a crib set up in my second bedroom. It's small, yeah, but it'll do for now.

And I have several bags of baby clothes all washed and ready to go. In neutral colors."

"You really don't want to know?" I open the passenger side door to my SUV and she slides in.

"You do?"

Yeah. Kind of.

I give her a nonchalant shrug before closing her door. "It's whatever you want, I guess."

"Ms. Lowe, if you'll just follow me, please." The nurse smiles from the doorway to the waiting room. She eyes me as I stand up and follow Tatum to her exam room and I see her brows furrow in confusion.

"This is the baby's father," Tatum explains. "Dex Foster."

The nurse's expression changes completely and it's clear she knows exactly who I am. Her smile grows and she shakes my hand. "It's a pleasure to meet you Mr. Foster. And congratulations on your pregnancy."

"Thank you." I clear my throat. "Uh, I'm sorry I have to ask this, but everything here is confidential, right?"

Tatum looks at me, surprised that I'm asking but the nurse nods. "Yes, Sir. Patient confidentiality is something we take very seriously here."

"I just uh..." I push my hand through my hair. "I want to make sure the press doesn't get wind of my being here with Tatum. Not for my sake but for hers. I don't want her to be bombarded by the media in these next few weeks if I can help it."

"Not at all, Sir. I can promise you, nothing will come from this office whatsoever. But just between us, I'm a huge fan. Go Red Tails." She winks with a smile and I somehow already feel a little more at ease. The nurse's eyes fall to Tatum's hand. She's clearly looking for a ring that isn't there and for some reason that makes my chest feel funny.

Tatum isn't my wife, but now I wonder how many people will see us together over the coming weeks, and certainly once the baby is born, and assume we're married. The idea of a wife and kids was never on my bingo card of life. I just assumed I would play hockey and randomly hookup with women whenever I wanted for the rest of my days. Now the idea of fucking an unfamiliar woman makes my stomach turn. It's a weird sensation that I push out of my mind in order to be all in for Tatum's appointment.

The nurse takes her vitals and then asks her to tuck her shirt under her bra and push her pants down just below her belly so there's enough room to do an ultrasound. Seated on Tatum's left, I look away at first, not sure of my place here as the man who put this child inside her but also a man she's not currently with. I know it's all for medical reasons, but it still feels a bit like I'm invading her privacy. When I turn back around, Tatum's bare belly is on full display. As the technician squirts a weird jelly on her stomach and then turns on the ultrasound machine, Tatum slides her hand out from the exam table waiting for me to take it. Instinctively, I reach out and fold my warm hand over her cold skin, giving her hand a gentle squeeze to let her know I'm right here with her.

Though I'm pretty sure she's holding my hand for me, not the other way around.

The machine the ultrasound tech uses looks like a small computer with a detachable wand and I watch as the technician slides it through the goop on Tatum's stomach and across her abdomen. She's quiet for a minute or two and then pushes a button near her computer that brings the speakers to life.

Our ears are filled with a constant whooshing sound.

Tatum smiles.

"Hear that?"

I nod. "Mmhmm."

"That's our baby, Dex." She squeezes my hand tight. "That's the baby's heartbeat."

That's our baby.

That sound.

My new favorite sound.

Bells and sirens when the puck enters the net.

Buzzers at the end of periods.

The snapping of cameras from the press.

Commentary from sportscasters.

The sound of my skates on the ice.

The slapping of sticks when they hit the puck.

Cheers from fans.

Those are the parts of my job I'm used to hearing. Sounds I rarely think about during the day, but ones that fill me with endless excitement and joy.

But this...

The soft sound of my baby's heartbeat.

This sound is on a whole new level.

There is nothing like it.

"Holy shit." My words are a whisper as I watch the technician move the wand around Tatum's stomach while soaking up the constant and quick little whooshing sound of the baby's heartbeat. An unexpected wave of euphoria flutters through my chest, my hand over my heart as I catch my breath. "That's our baby."

"Yeah." Tatum smiles.

"And here's your baby, right here." The technician points to the tiny body on the black screen that vaguely resembles a small human.

This is unreal.

"I can't believe it. My little Tater Tot."

A light burst of sweet laughter comes from Tatum. "Tater Tot."

I snap my eyes to her. "Is that okay? I'm sorry. I can call it some—"

"No." She shakes her head, her eyes watering. "It's perfect."

Tatum Lowe is carrying my child inside her. A child so small and perfect and unscathed by the cruel world around it. That we created something so perfect together in one night of unadulterated lust, a perfectness that will forever change our lives, blows my mind.

A baby!

My baby!

Our baby!

Swallowing a lump of emotions creeping up my throat, my eyes steal another glance at Tatum. Tears slip down her cheek and a wondrously breathtaking smile crosses her face as she watches the screen off to her right and it's this moment right here, I want to preserve.

The moment I behold the mother of my child and know without a doubt in the world, I will do whatever it takes to make her happy. I'll bend over backwards to protect her and our child at all costs.

They're my life now.

I want this more than I've ever wanted anything.

I know we don't know each other beyond the bedroom, but there's something inside that makes me feel at peace knowing our lives are forever woven together now.

We can do this.

I want to do this.

I want to do this with Tatum.

Taking her hand in my own, I give it a light squeeze and lean over to kiss her forehead. "Look at that, Tate. We did that. We made that."

The black little blob kicks its leg on the screen and I gasp. "Holy shit!" I want so badly to place my hand on Tatum's belly but it has goop all over it. "Can you feel that? Did the baby just kick you?"

The technician chuckles. "That was definitely a kick, yes. And I'm certain Mommy felt that one."

Tatum giggles. "Yep. I most certainly did."

"Do you guys know the sex of the baby yet?"

"No," Tatum says. "And I kind of don't want to know."

The technician smiles. "Okay. Then I won't try to get baby to move so we can see."

"Thank you," Tatum says, wiping a few tears from her cheek. "I think I just want it to be a surprise." She squeezes my hand, looking over at me with a timid smile. I give her hand a reassuring squeeze right back.

Whatever she wants.

Whatever she needs.

The technician finishes her scans and prints us a picture of the next generation's star hockey player, that's what I'm calling him anyway. Holding the picture in my hand, I smile, remembering the moment Zeke showed us all Elsie's ultrasound picture and how proud and excited he was to show her off.

"I can't wait to show this to the guys. And Rory. Oh, my God, she'll flip." I turn back toward Tatum as she cleans herself up, my smile faltering. "She's probably already seen one, hasn't she?"

Tatum gives me a sympathetic look. "Yeah. She umm, she's been with me for each one so far."

Fucking Rory.

"I've never been so jealous of my sister in all my life."

If only I had known.

"I'm so sorry, Dex."

"No, don't apologize." I kiss the back of her hand. "None of this is your fault. Or mine. It just is what it is."

"For what it's worth, she's been so great to have around. My strongest support person."

"This does not surprise me, knowing my sister. But just so you know, if it comes to a choice between me or her to hold our baby, I will plow her down without regret to get to my kid."

Tatum laughs. "I have no doubt that's exactly what would happen."

"In all seriousness though, you'll have me, Tate. I promise you'll have me for anything you need."

She locks eyes with me for a moment and smiles, not saying anything. For a fleeting moment I fear she doesn't want me to be here for her. Maybe she doesn't want me involved and those thoughts bring on a whole new form of self-doubt and disappointment. I step across the room to reach for the door when she stops me.

"Hey Dex?"

"Yeah?" I turn around to see her head tilted, her smile fading. "You not feeling well?"

"I'm glad it's you, Dex."

"What?"

"If I had to have a kid with a random guy I barely know." She shrugs lightly. "I'm really glad it's you."

Well shit.

I did not expect to hear that.

Nor did I expect my chest to tighten and my throat to close.

How does she take my breath away with just a few simple words?

Stepping towards her, I push my hand through her hair, bringing her forehead to my lips. I linger there just a little longer than I probably should, squeezing my eyes closed and remembering how she felt in my arms several months ago. And how she feels now.

"I'm glad it's you too, Tatum."

12

TATUM

DEX

Did you know your partner can experience pregnancy symptoms right along with you? It's like some kind of magic voodoo shit.

ME

Is this your way of trying to tell me your breasts are growing too?

DEX

You want to feel them and find out? 😏

ME

GIF of Ron Swanson giving deadpan expression

DEX

checks out chest in the mirror Nah. I'm good. But I swear I'm eating more. You're eating for two. I think I'm eating for all three of us.

ME

You know you're a pro hockey player, right? Playing more = eating more.

DEX

Maybe so.

ME

Come talk to me when you can't sleep because you have crazy dreams or you're peeing all the time because apparently bladders fail to exist in pregnant women. If only I had a penis, I could just whip it out, pee in a cup, and move on with my day.

DEX

That's only a slightly disturbing mental picture.

DEX

I know you told me you don't really follow hockey, but do you know anything about the sport?

ME

I like reading hockey romance books. Does that count? The guys in those books are always hot as hell, and there are scenes where they play the game.

DEX

So, you read hockey porn. That's it? Never been to a game?

ME

Couple times as a kid I think. And what makes you think I read porn? I said romance.

DEX

gives you knowing stare Have you ever gotten off reading one of those books, Tate?

ME

I'm not answering that.

DEX

See? Porn. I'm not judging. One of my teammates reads a lot of romance. He may or may not have recommended it to some of us. Whatever makes you feel good. But it's nothing like real hockey. You should come to a game sometime. I'll get you tickets.

ME

I mean I get scoring touchdowns is important but hot sweaty men on skates who are beasts on the ice, and, if you're any indication, lovers off the ice? Yes please. That's a thirst trap I'll not turn away from.

DEX

GIF of cat shaking head no No Tate. Just no.

ME

What?

DEX

There are no fucking touchdowns in Hockey. They are goals. Dear God, you're going to need a tutorial.

133

ME

Whatever. Puck in the hole equals points. I get it.

DEX

GIF of Ryan Reynolds face palm Pucks go in the net Tate. No holes in hockey. Well...unless you're shooting for the five hole.

ME

?? What the hell's a five hole? That sounds kind of dirty.

DEX

LOL! What can I say? Hockey is a dirty sport.

ME

A sexy sport though. So much more than football.

DEX

That's something we can agree on.

ME

I can't believe I got knocked up by a hockey player.

DEX

The sexiest hockey player to ever exist too. Let's make sure that's clear.

ME

Wow. Will our kid be as humble as you too? 😜

DEX

Of course. He'll have to get that from you though.

DEX

How are you feeling?

ME

What's that? I can't hear you over the massive amounts of peeing I'm doing today.

DEX

Is your classroom next to a bathroom?

ME

If by next to, you mean on the opposite end of the building, then yes. Yes, it is.

DEX

☹ Sorry to hear that. I could order one of those portable toilets like they have in hospitals and nursing homes.

ME

Because that's what I need in front of a classroom of first graders. *face palm emoji*

DEX

Okay. Maybe not. How are you feeling otherwise?

ME

I'm good.

DEX

Just good?

ME

Yep.

DEX

There's nothing else?

ME

Do you want there to be something else?

DEX

Uh...I'm just checking in on you.

ME

You don't need to do that.

DEX

I disagree. Checking in on you is my job.

ME

Negative. Defending your goalie is your job as is putting a puck in someone else's net.

DEX

Glares at your baby bump Looks like I already put a puck in someone else's net. 😏

ME

Oh, for fuck's sake.

DEX

Yes. Yes, it was for fuck's sake. On your vacay bucket list, remember? And if I do say so myself, I remember it being pretty damn good.

ME

Goodnight Dex.

DEX

Goodnight Tatum.

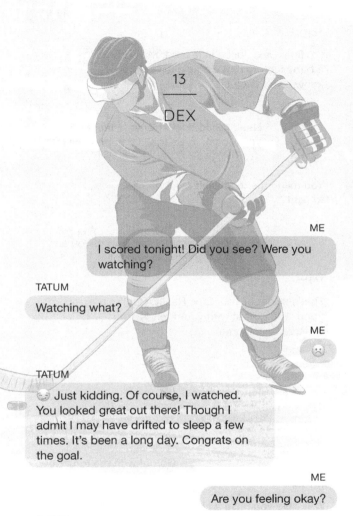

13
—
DEX

ME

I scored tonight! Did you see? Were you watching?

TATUM

Watching what?

ME

😣

TATUM

😊 Just kidding. Of course, I watched. You looked great out there! Though I admit I may have drifted to sleep a few times. It's been a long day. Congrats on the goal.

ME

Are you feeling okay?

TATUM

You just won another game...a game in which you scored...and you're asking if I'm feeling okay?

ME

Tate...

TATUM

I'm fine, Dex. Just a little tired. My body is a baby factory that works overtime you know. Tired is okay.

ME

Need me to come rub your feet or give you a back massage? I can bring snacks.

TATUM

You mean the team isn't celebrating tonight?

ME

Yeah, they are, but I can skip it. You and the baby are more important.

TATUM

That's sweet of you, Dex. Really. But I'm good. You go out with your friends. You deserve to celebrate.

ME

Tate...

TATUM

I promise I'm okay, Dex.

ME

Go out with me tomorrow.

TATUM

Why? Do you have a charity thing or something?

> **ME**
>
> No. I have the day off tomorrow and was just hoping to spend some time with you. Thought about introducing you to my guys on the team. I guess that was my way of asking you out. Sorry, I'm not very good at this. Don't worry about it. Maybe another time.

> **TATUM**
>
> I would love to go.

> **ME**
>
> Wait. Really?

> **TATUM**
>
> ☺ Yes. Really.

> **ME**
>
> Okay. I'll pick you up at three?

> **TATUM**
>
> See you then. G'night, Dex.

> **ME**
>
> Night Tatum.

"I should uh, apologize or whatever ahead of time for anything said here tonight." I press on the Ring doorbell at Milo's front door.

She chuckles beside me. "That bad, huh?"

"I love 'em like brothers and we all act like brothers, sooo..."

"Oh, I get it." She nods. "Lots of pissing contests and an abundance of dick talk?"

"That pretty much sums it up, yeah. In our locker room you see more foreskins than a Rabbi during a baby boom." I laugh. "God, we're so predictable."

She giggles. "Nah. Just men. Teammates. Athletes. I get it. My brother played baseball in high school. It's all I ever heard from his friends when they were around."

"Whatever he says, don't believe him!" says a voice from the doorbell speaker. "Dex's dick is the smallest one on the team."

I cock my head and roll my eyes. "Uh, she's seen my dick, asshole. Pretty sure she knows better."

Tatum pushes me out of the way of the doorbell camera with a smirk. "Whoa! I don't know anything though! I mean if his is the smallest, I'm all for meeting the rest of you! Do we need to have a dick-off or something?"

Loud female cackles come from the other side of the door before it swings open and Tatum is greeted with a huge hug from Carissa and Charlee. "Oh, my God, Hi! I'm Charlee and this is Carissa and I think we're all now best friends!"

Tatum laughs but hugs them all just the same. "I could use a few new best friends for sure! Hi. I'm Tatum!"

"It's soooo good to mee you, Tatum," Carissa sings. "Also, look how fucking adorable you look! EEEEK!" She hits my bicep playfully. "Can you even believe that's your kid in there?"

Tatum turns to me with a smirk and a nod toward Carissa. "This one might give Rory a run for her money."

I roll my eyes. "Just wait till they're all three together.

It's like a fuckin' hen fest in here listening to them squeal and snicker about one thing or another."

"It's your dick sizes, Dex," Charlee explains. "We're always laughing about your dick sizes."

"Yeah, and Colb says yours is pierced! When do we get to see that?"

Colby shakes his head. "Whoa, whoa, whoa. I never said anything about you seeing it, Smalls."

Tatum's eyes grow and she gasps. "Oh, my God, that's right!" She shoots her hand up in the air. "I can certainly confirm the piercing!" She grins at the ladies. "So, I'm guessing piercings aren't a team thing?"

Charlee laughs. "No, but they sure as hell should be!" She turns to Milo. "Why don't you get pierced, babe?"

"Because nobody touches my man hammer but you, Goldilocks."

"Goldilocks?" Tatum's brow furrows, but Charlee waves her off.

"Long story."

"Bro, man hammer?" I cringe. "Nah man. I think we can come up with something a little stronger than man hammer."

The girls lead Tatum inside while the guys follow behind.

"How about lap rocket?" Zeke suggests.

Quinton shakes his head. "Clam Clogger."

Colby winks. "Thrill drill."

"No way." Hawken shakes his head. "Mine's Long Dong Silver."

"I think I prefer purple-headed yogurt slinger." I nod, happy with my thought.

"Charlee called mine Fuck Norris the other day and I don't hate it." Milo smirks and we all laugh as we meet up with the ladies in the kitchen. I go through and introduce her to each of the guys and then stand back and watch as she takes each one of them in and gets to know something about each of them individually.

Not intimidated or scared of them at all.

Like none of us are professional hockey players with million-dollar salaries.

Because she's amazing like that.

"Did your parents never lie to you when you were a kid?" Carissa asks the group over dinner. We were just chatting about what fibs we'll tell our child as its growing up.

"Pfft. All the fucking time. Like I said, my parents weren't good role models growing up. Thank God, Rory and I had each other."

"My parents used to tell me fibs all the time when I was young," she says. "Some of them took me an embarrassingly long time to figure out they were in fact, lies."

"You mean like Santa Claus and the Tooth Fairy?" Zeke asks.

"Oh no." She giggles. "Much worse. Like for one, my dad used to tell us it was illegal to turn the light on in the back seat of the car at night, so my siblings and I never touched it. Not once."

Charlee giggles. "Oh, you poor sweet thing."

"Hey Colby, remember what your dad used to say about those ice cream trucks?" Milo smiles.

"Oh shit, yeah. He used to tell us when the ice cream truck plays music around the neighborhood it's letting you know it's empty and has to go restock."

I slap my palm to my forehead. "Oh man, you fell for that?"

"Yep. Sure did."

"Soooo I have two." Tatum beams. She is very much enjoying this conversation and I am very much enjoying watching her.

"My whole life, I thought Hansel and Gretel got eaten by the witch!"

Okay that one makes me cackle. "No, you did not."

She raises her hand. "Swear to God. I thought the whole story was a cautionary tale about not running away from your parents. It took until I was twenty-two! Twenty freaking two before I actually read the whole book and realized that is not, in fact, how it ends."

Charlee throws her head back in laughter. "Oh shit, that's funny!"

"That's not the worst one."

"Oh no!" Carissa leans forward, her chin resting in her hands. "This ought to be good. Do tell."

Tatum holds her forehead with the tips of her fingers. "Oh, God, I can't believe I fell for this one."

"Wait, let me guess." I stop her.

She shakes her head. "You'll never guess but go ahead and try."

"Umm was it if you swallow gum, it'll never digest?"

"Nope."

"If you swim after eating, you'll get a stomachache?"

"Nope."

"The parks aren't closed when Mom has a headache?"

"Huh?"

My shoulders fall. "Yeah, that's what my mom always said."

Tatum chuckles. "You poor thing...but also, nope."

"Alright, I give up."

She takes a deep breath and tries to wipe the smile from her face. "Okay, here goes. So, my mom used to suffer from nightmares."

We all nod as she explains.

"And I mean like, a lot of them. And when she had nightmares, she would uh...you know, scream and moan and be loud, and I would lie in my bed at night and feel bad for her because she couldn't get herself to wake up from her nightmares."

"Oh fuck..."

I think I see where this is going.

"Yeah." She nods, her eyes widening. "So, one night I go to the bathroom and when I'm walking back from the bathroom to my room, my parents' bedroom door is open and all I see is my dad's bare butt on top of my mother!"

There's a collective sucking in of lips around the table to hold back our laughter, because yep, I was right about where this is going.

"Tatum!"

She turns toward Carissa. "And there I was thinking... wow! Dad is trying to get my mom to wake up from her nightmare. Weird that he's not wearing pajamas but how nice of him to help Mom."

I can't help it. I burst out laughing as does everyone around this table, and thank God Tatum is laughing too. "Oh stop! This is too much!"

"Dex, it took until I was in high school to realize my mother was in fact not having nightmares and they just liked to fuck. And it took until I was in college to ever say something about it." She laughs. "And now that night is a core memory for me that I will never ever, *ever* be able to get rid of, or unsee!"

I'm holding my stomach from laughing so hard. "Oh fuck, Tatum. That's the best story I think I've ever heard in my whole damn life. I'm so sorry."

"No, you're not, you ass." She slaps me playfully on my arm. "You're getting off on my misfortunate childhood."

"Hey, it's not my fault you were a sweet naïve little girl...teenager...young adult. Twenty-two, huh?"

"Shut up." She huffs out a giggle and I can't hold back. She's so damn cute. Her smile...I think I could get off on her smile alone. She has been so much fun hanging out with all of us. I find myself dreading having to take her home. I'd give anything to prolong our time together.

"Two truths and a lie." Tatum pulls her spoon from her mouth, having devoured the ice cream she just slipped inside. At her insistence, we picked up a couple pints of ice cream after leaving Milo's and I invited her back to my place since it was closer to the store than her place. Nobody likes melted ice cream. Hers is mint chocolate chip. I chose chocolate marshmallow. "See you if you can tell which one is a lie."

Easy peasy.

"Alright."

"Umm...I have four siblings. I make a spectacular coconut cream pie. The first concert I ever went to was Kenny G."

An amused grin spread across my face. "Kenny G?"

"Mhmm."

"Has to be that one."

She winces. "Oooh sorry, but you're wrong."

"Seriously? Kenny G? He's that saxophone elevator music guy, right?"

"Yep. My dad loved him back in the day. Had all his albums. When he came to town, he bought tickets for the whole family. I was eight. And literally all the audience members were old people. I was the youngest person in the room."

I shake my head. "Wow. And you didn't walk out of there itching to learn the saxophone."

She grins, a pinkness coming to her cheeks. "It's what I played in my high school band."

"Ha! The visuals I now have of little Tatum Lowe in her band uniform."

"I know. So hot, right?"

"So, which of the other two was the lie?"

She scrunches her nose. "I can't stand coconut cream pie and I've never made one in my life."

"You're a very convincing liar."

"You think so?" She grins and something in my chest does this little flippy thing.

"Yeah. So, you have four siblings then?"

She nods with excitement. "Yeah, I do. They're great. We're all very close. Simeon, he's the oldest. He's a veterinarian with his own practice in Lansing. My brother Shane is a plastics engineer. My third brother, Silas is about to graduate from grad school with his master's in chemistry, then there's my sister Tess. She's an artist. And then me."

"Wow, busy family. And you get to see them often?"

She nods and then shrugs. "Yeah. Well, I did. We were all within an hour of each other. But now, not so much. I'm the one who decided to move away. I have a feeling my sister might follow me out here. Chicago is a way better place for her to grow as an artist than anywhere in Michigan, but I think she's waiting it out to see how I like it here."

"So clearly the family knows about us? The baby, I mean? Our baby?"

Shit, it feels weird asking someone that question.

"Mhmm. I called my mom shortly after I found out. She's always been such a huge supporter of me. And there was no way I could keep it a secret from my family unless I plan to never see them again. Besides, once Tess knows something, the whole family knows. She's the only sister I have. We tell each other everything, so…"

"Ah. I understand."

I really want to ask her what she told them about me, but how the hell do I ask that?

Hey, did you tell them a rich and famous hockey player knocked you up?

Would they consider that a good thing or a horrible thing?

Do you tell them you liked me or did you tell them we don't speak?

Do they know I'm taking responsibility?

Do they know I want to be involved in our kid's life?

Do they hate me for what I did to their daughter?

Suddenly, a horrific thought crosses my mind and my stomach drops.

Will her family ask her to move back home?

Will they encourage her to fight me for sole custody?

Fuck.

What do I do if that happens?

Can she take my kid away so I can never see it again?

Would she really do that?

"You're turn." She nudges my knee with her own.

14

TATUM

"Two truths and a lie. Let's hear it."

"Oh uh...okay."

Reaching over, Dex slips his hand under my calf and lifts my leg, setting it down on his thigh, and then wraps his hand around my foot. He digs his fingers into my arch massaging my foot and it is everything. It feels so good I have to stop myself from moaning. Though I wonder how he would react if I did. The thought almost makes me giggle.

"Let's see. Um, I know every word of every Taylor Swift song ever written."

No way.

Every single one?

"I know how to knit."

Hmm...possible? But unlikely.

"And I've been skating on ice since I was six."

Well that one is clearly true.

I narrow my eyes and watch the good-looking man on

the other end of my couch for any clue to the correct answer, but he gives nothing away.

"Oooh, that's a hard one. I don't know if I can picture you knitting, but then again...something about you makes me think of course, you know how to knit. You've clearly been skating for a long time, so I'm going to say you're lying about the T. Swift songs."

He tilts his head giving me his best sympathetic expression. "I'm sorry, Tater but you're wrong. You give me a title, I can sing you any Swifty song out there."

I laugh. "No kidding?"

"I would never lie about my BFF, Swift."

"You know her?"

Oh my God, if he knows her personally, I might just die right here, right now!

"Nah, I don't know her personally. She's my pregame routine. I dance out to her music every game day."

I bite down on my lips to keep from laughing and study him for a moment. Maybe he's lying about that and maybe he's not. Either way, "Watching Dex Foster dance it out in a locker room to Taylor Swift is now my newest bucket list item."

Squeezing my foot in his hand, he winks. "Guess you'll have to come to a game sometime to make that happen."

"Oh, is that a promise?"

"Sweetheart, I think I would promise you anything."

Whoa!

Does he know he said that out loud?

Did he mean to say it?

My cheeks flush and my eyes glaze and I'm somehow hyper aware of his hand now wrapped around my other foot, his fingers sending tiny electric jolts through my toes.

"So good," I think to myself.

"What's so good?"

"What?"

Oh, my God.

He smirks. "You said 'So good.'"

"I...did I?"

Nice going Tatum.

You said that out loud!

Way to sound like a perv.

"You did."

"Shit, I'm sorry." I palm my forehead and shake my head at the same time, nervous laughter floating out of my mouth. "I didn't mean for that to sound so...ugh, I was just thinking...you know, it feels good. My feet, I mean. I haven't had a foot rub in a long time."

"Good. I'm glad it's helping."

An awkward silence falls between us as he continues his caress on my feet. I could get lost in watching his hands manipulate my body, moving my foot this way and that, his fingers gripping, sliding, rubbing, stimulating.

God!

Get it together, Tatum!

"Your lie then," I say changing the subject. "You don't know how to knit?"

"Oh, I know how to knit. I've been knitting for the last few months, actually."

"Sooo he sings Taylor Swift and knows how to knit? Who even are you, Dex Foster?"

His magnetic eyes penetrate mine. "Just a nobody

hockey player." He grins. "One who didn't learn to skate until he was ten."

I hear the humor in his voice but I'm stuck on the fact he thinks so little of himself.

"A nobody hockey player, huh?"

"Mhmm."

"A nobody hockey player who makes millions? A nobody hockey player who donates his time and money to a community sports program for underprivileged kids?"

His brow perks up. "You checkin' up on me Tate?"

"Maybe. But a nobody hockey player is where I must disagree with you. I think you're much more than a nobody, Mr. Foster." I smooth my hand over my growing baby bump. "And in a few short months you'll be the dad of the cutest little hockey fan in the league."

As I speak, there's a movement underneath my hand that makes me smile. It's one of the weirdest but best feelings in the entire world.

"The baby's moving!"

His eyes grow as they land on my stomach and he watches as this baby does what feels like a somersault inside me.

"Good God it looks like you have an alien in there. That shouldn't be normal."

I chuckle and grab his hand, placing it on my stomach. He swallows hard and glances at me before focusing on the part of me he's touching. We sit in awkward silence waiting for any sign of movement and then finally it happens again.

"Holy shit. I can feel that," Dex exclaims.

"Yeah." That's all I can say because I'm too busy smiling.

"Does that hurt?" He blanches. "When the baby moves inside you?"

I shake my head. "Not usually. Every now and then he or she kicks my rib or bounces a little too hard near my bladder. It doesn't really hurt as much as it can get uncomfortable once in a while. It's not like there's room to stretch out in there."

"This is amazing."

I spend the next few minutes leaning back on the couch allowing Dex to roam his warm hand over my stomach chasing baby movements. I close my eyes for a quick second, relaxing in the warmth of Dex's proximity and the gentleness of his touch. When I open them again, he's watching me. His pupils dilated, his stare hungry as he glances between my eyes and my mouth.

My lips separate and my breath catches and all I can think about is what it would feel like to have his lips on mine again. I swiftly moisten my lips with my tongue and watch as his Adam's apple bobs along his neck when he swallows. My heart rate rises and nerves flutter through my whole body. Dex moves his hand across my stomach one more time and it's all I can do not to moan. His touch feels amazing and I'm clearly extra hormonal and horny because I would give anything for him to drop his hand between my legs and relieve me of this sudden tension.

"Dex," I breathe.

"I should get you home." He pulls away from me and rises from the couch.

Wait. What?

No!

He starts to walk away, toward the front door, which

isn't far, and I spring from the couch as well. I mean, as much as a super pregnant woman can spring.

"Oh, okay." I walk with him, fighting my internal disappointment. "Hey, I had a really great time with you, Dex. Thank you for today. And...you know, the ice cream and the foot massage."

"You're welcome," he mumbles as he slides his shoes on.

Why does he seem so tense now?

Did I say something to upset him?

A few minutes ago, he was in awe over our baby moving and now? It's like his mood just snapped. He reaches for the doorknob when I finally speak up again.

"Dex, what's wrong?"

"Nothi—"

"Did I do something? Say something wrong? I'm sorry I—"

He turns. His eyes squeezed tightly closed like he's in pain. I'm about to ask him what I can do when his eyes open again and he's on me like a lion to its prey. His whole hand against the side of my face, his lips crash against mine and he's kissing me with a fury I haven't felt since...well, since that night together in May. He sweeps his tongue across my lips, begging me to open, and I welcome his intrusion.

"Tatum." My name is on his breath, his whisper of a voice fueling the desire pooling between my legs. I don't know if we should be doing this but when the man who gave me the absolutely best sex of my life is standing in his apartment kissing me, who am I to even consider stopping him? His mouth is demanding against mine and I ache to please him. To give him everything he wants from me.

I've wanted Dex since the moment I saw him standing in his kitchen. I wanted him the night I walked out of his resort room and I dreamed of the day I might get to have this experience with him again.

"Dex. Please," I beg in between swipes of his tongue.

"I'm sorry, Tate," he whispers against my lips, refusing to stop his assault on my lips. "I know we shouldn't be doing this, but I...fuck!"

"I want this, Dex. Please. I need you."

He pulls back, weighing his options, staring at me like I'm painful to look at. I fear whatever I might say could scare him off but I tell him what I'm thinking anyway. At this point I would take a pity quickie. Anything to relieve this tension.

"I can't reach between my legs anymore, Dex. I need help. Help me."

Dex's eyes bulge as he watches me try to touch myself and then he snaps.

"Tatum," he growls, kissing me harder, bruising my lips. "You have no idea how much I've thought about you during these past months. You and your sweet dripping pussy. Fuck, you were magnificent." He slides his hand into my leggings and slips two fingers under my panties between my legs.

"Oooh, God, yes." My head falls back and I groan loudly as he swipes through me and grunts against my mouth. "Fuuuuuck, Tate. You're soaked for me." He pulls his hand out and sucks those two wet fingers into his

SUSAN RENEE

mouth, his eyes never leaving mine. "More. I need to taste you."

"Yes, please."

His strong hand wraps around me and he lifts me easily into his arms. He carries me down a dark hallway and into the last room on the left. His bedroom. There, he lays me down gently, my hips at the edge of his bed. Slowly he slides my leggings and black panties down my legs, pulling them off entirely and tossing them to the floor.

"Are you comfortable like this? You okay?"

Gah! How sweet of him to consider me.

I nod. "Yes. Yes, I'm fine. I promise."

Kneeling in front of me, he rests my legs on his shoulders and peppers my inner thighs with sweet kisses. My bottom lip between my teeth, I prop myself up onto my elbows and watch him.

"So beautiful, Tate. So fucking beautiful." And before I can respond to his compliments, he's swiping his tongue through me from ass to clit and I'm a goner.

"Ooooh fuuuuuck yes. Just like that."

He spreads me wide open, his tongue licking, mouth sucking, teeth biting.

"Dex, please," I breathe. "More."

"Guide me, baby. Use me. Take what you need."

I have never in my entire adult life had a man tell me to use him and take whatever I need from him so when Dex offers, I refuse to think twice about chasing my screamy dream. It's been over seven months since I've seen any action and dammit, I deserve a night of pleasure. I reach down and tug at his hair, his moan against me spurring me on as I thrust against his mouth.

156

"Fucking hell, Tatum. You are so goddamn hot. Fuck my face, baby. Let me taste you as you come over my mouth."

"Dex!" I cry out, moving faster, harder against him. He juts out his tongue, licking me, swirling against me as I ride his face until my body begins to tremble and I'm about to meet my maker. He reaches up and pushes two fingers gently inside me, curling them up against my inner wall and I scream so loud my throat is sore.

"Ooooh, my GOD! YES! YES! YES! UNGHHH!"

Dex doesn't stop his onslaught. Instead, he laps up every drop of me he can, licking his lips and wiping his chin before he kisses his way up my body, tenderly kissing my mouth. With ease, he lies down next to me and pulls me against him, my head lying in the crook of his shoulder. It's comfortable here.

"Thank you, Dex."

Those are the last words I remember murmuring to him before my body betrays me. I don't wake again until morning.

DEX

Holy shit Tate! Did you know 1 in every 2000 babies is born with teeth? TEETH! Our kid can be born with teeth! Why does that give me visions of a monster baby literally eating its way out of you??? Hawken is slightly horrified.

ME

Where do you think guys learn to eat pussy in the first place? 😏

DEX

😮 Is that...wait...no. You're fucking with me. Goddamn it Tate!

ME

LOL! Oh God, I can't laugh or I'll have to pee.

DEX

How about Thor?

ME

Only if the middle name can be Cletus?

DEX

WTF? Thor Cletus Foster? I just threw up in my mouth. No way.

ME

How about Violet?

DEX

Are we having a girl??? Did you find out without me?

ME

No. But you seem so confident that it's a boy. Thought I would change it up.

DEX

It is a boy. I can just feel it. This kid is going to be the next generation's biggest hockey star.

ME

And you could tell that as you were pile driving into me? That all your little swimmers were boys?

DEX

Hell yeah! I Think that might be my superpower! I can mass produce tiny, microscopic dicks! And I didn't hear you complaining about me driving into you. Pretty sure your words were something like "Oh God...don't stop...so good..."

DEX

....

DEX

....

DEX

Speechless huh? That's what I thought.

"Yeah, Baby. Just like that. Spread those legs for me. I want to feast on that sweet pussy. That's my good girl."

I watch as Dex's head lowers between her legs, his tongue running along her soft pink center and circling around her clit. She moans loudly, writhing beneath him. Her eyes squeezed closed as she focuses on her pleasure.

"So fucking good, Baby. Fuck, I'm drunk on your pussy. Always so ready for me."

"Yesssss," she sighs. *"More. I want more, Dex. Need more."* She grabs onto his hair and pushes him back down between her legs and he continues to pleasure her.

"Dex? Why are you doing this?" I don't understand why I'm here. Why am I being forced to watch this? I can't even figure out who the woman he's with is but my heart breaks with every pass of his tongue.

That should be me.

He should be with me.

Why isn't he with me?

Dex circles his tongue over and over again, sucking, licking, nipping, and she's coming like a freight train. Her arousal spread over his mouth and chin. He stands with a victorious smile.

"That's my good girl. You are fucking delicious."

He lifts her legs until they're resting on his shoulders and then palms his cock, sliding it between her legs and lining himself up.

"Dex, please!" I whisper. "Please don't do this."

He sinks himself deep inside her and I watch in horror as his head falls back in ecstasy and he groans that deep sexy groan I've heard before.

"Fucking perfect for me."

"Dex!"

My eyes shoot open with the sound of my alarm, but the twinge in my chest doesn't go away. The uncomfortable feeling is coupled with a despair that leaves my mouth dry and my eyes ready to spill over with unshed tears. It takes me a few minutes to calm my nerves and realize I was just dreaming, because hell, did it feel one hundred percent real. I was right there. I was in the room. I watched him pleasure her. I looked on as she soaked it all in and it nearly crippled me to hear him tell her how perfect she was for him. I stare up at my ceiling trying to figure out what the hell is wrong with my brain right now.

Why am I having sex dreams?

I never have sex dreams.

I don't understand why it wasn't me Dex was with in my dream.

Why was I forced to watch him with someone else?

And why did it hurt so goddamn much?

"Fucking pregnancy brain," I mumble, rolling out of bed and making my way to the bathroom. "Nope. Nope. Nope. This is all your fault so kindly fuck off and eat a bag of dicks. I don't have time for this right now."

Yeah.

That'll tell my stupid body who's boss.

"No more wild sex dreams of Dex with other women. I don't need a heart attack before this baby comes."

Grabbing my phone from its charger, I turn on one of my many good-morning playlists and crank up the volume. With any luck my favorite songs will drown out all my other thoughts and allow me to focus on my day ahead.

"Hey, good morning, Mama." Rory springs into my classroom looking like the perfect Kindergarten teacher with her bright red dress with yellow polka dots and her hair pulled up in two messy buns. Her black Vans bring the entire look together. Rory Foster is a whole vibe on such a bleak January day, and she makes me smile every time I see her.

"Morning, Rory."

"How ya feeling?"

I nod with a light shrug. "I think I'm okay. A rough morning but once I got here, I was able to keep my mind off of things."

"Uh oh, what things?"

I wave her off. "Oh, it's nothing. Not important."

"Of course, it's important." She sits on one of the tables in front of my desk and folds her hands in her lap. "Tell me all the things. What's eating you?"

You mean who's eating me?

Does she know that...?

Nah. Siblings don't share that stuff.

Right?

You really probably don't want to know this.

"All of the things," she emphasizes, giving me a come at me gesture. "Let's hear it."

I let out a quick breath and cock my head. "I had a sex dream last night."

Her eyes bulge. "Oooooh is this some sort of horny pregnant woman thing? Do you have sex dreams a lot? Get it girl!"

My cheeks flush. "No, I don't. I never have sex dreams."

She leans forwards and murmurs, "Were you getting railed? Was it every woman's wet dream?"

I cringe. "Well...I mean, probably not yours."

Her shoulders fall and her smile falters. "What? Why no—ooooh." She cringes. "You had a Dex sex dream?"

Oh my God, this is so uncomfortable. "Yeah...but also no."

"Huh?"

"Okay, so ugh...I can't believe I'm saying this."

"Hey, he's my brother. If anyone should be uncomfortable here it's me. Just lay it on me. I can handle it." She twists her mouth. "I think."

"Okay so in my dream it was Dex and some other woman I don't know."

"And you?" She perks up. "Like a threesome?"

I shake my head. "No. Just the two of them. And I'm the outsider looking in. Forced to watch them together. It was super..." I sigh. "Well, I woke up feeling angry and heartbroken. I mean what the fuck is that about?"

"Heartbroken because you weren't the woman he was with?"

"Yeah, I guess so."

A grin spreads across her face like the Grinch who stole Christmas. "You want to sleep with my brother!"

I gesture to my growing stomach. "Pretty sure I already took care of that."

"Hmm, true. Maybe you're just horny? I know that happens because Shelly used to talk about it all the time. Her husband was a lucky man for a few weeks."

"Yeah. Maybe you're right. It was just a weird way to wake up."

"I bet." She's quiet for a moment and then finally asks, "Sooo, are you and Dex a thing? Like officially?"

Does eating pussy make us official?
I don't think it does.
I probably shouldn't tell her that.

"We haven't really talked about it so, I guess that answer is no."

She rolls her eyes. "I'm gonna have to have a talk with that boy."

I huff out a quiet laugh. "It's really okay. If it's not meant to be, we'll find a parenting path we can both feel good about."

"You will. And you know if there's anything I can do, all you have to do is ask."

"Thank you, Rory."

She hops down from the table she was sitting on. "Hey, and while it's on my mind. Next Friday, Red Tails play at home. You're coming. You can sit with Charlee and Carissa and me. The WAGS, if you will."

"WAGS?"

"Wives and girlfriends of the players...and sisters I guess, since I'm there sometimes." She waves. "I'll shoot you more info later!"

I call after her. "But I'm not his girlfr—"

"See ya, Tate!" She's down the hall but I still hear her giggle.

"Ms. Lowe! Tyson just said I farted and tried to smell my butt!" I look up from my desk to find one of my little first grade buddies, Daniel, stomping toward me from across the room. I swear winter days are the worst. Poor kids can't get outside and let go of some energy so they'll bicker about literally anything. Apparently today it's farts.

"That's because he farted!" Tyson argues, following close behind.

Daniel gestures to him. "Yeah, but he just put his face near my butt to smell my butt."

I narrow my eyes at Tyson and try to choke back my laugh at the same time. "Tyson, did you really do that?"

"Yeah."

"Why would you do that, Bud?"

"To smell if he farted. That's why."

Can I really argue with that?

The kid had a hypothesis and he did the research.

"Alright well, I think maybe we should stick to our own personal spaces, Tyson. Sometimes farts just happen and that's okay."

"Yeah," Daniel pipes up. "My mom farted last night at supper and it was super loud. My dad gave her a high five."

"Well, that's...something, Daniel. How about you two finish your game over there because it's almost time for recess to be over and we'll have to clean up."

Daniel and Tyson gasp, beaming at each other like they totally forgot they were even playing together in the first place, and run off to their corner of the room leaving me to contemplate what it might be like raising a little boy.

Raising a little boy with Dex Foster.

As the kids play in their last few minutes of recess, I let my mind wander back to that night with Dex in his resort room. He was right in his text the other day. About wanting someone to hook up with while I was there. I wanted to sleep with someone who would rock my world for just one night. Someone who could show me what I missed out on all those years with my ex.

And Dex was one hundred percent that guy.

And to add the cherry on top of my Dex Foster Sundae, he was kind. He was friendly and he was irrevocably focused on me and the pleasure he knew he could give me.

And did he ever give it to me.

My eyes roll back as I feel him touching me, slipping his fingers between my legs. His breath on my neck, his lips on my skin.

"Fucking dripping for me, Babe.

Goddamn, I can't wait to be inside you.

Come on. Give it up for me."

I squeeze my thighs together trying to remember the feeling of his pressure. The fullness. The—

RIIIIIING

The sound of the recess bell brings me back to reality, seated at my desk, my hand on my chest almost cupping my throat. My heart is racing.

God that felt so real.

It was real.

Once upon a time.

But things are different now, and like it or not, these pregnancy hormones will have to settle themselves because Dex and I are not together in that way.

We're two people having a baby together and that's it.

With the exception of the other night, he hasn't expressed interest otherwise and I can respect that. Dex has a lot on his plate with his career. It would be selfish to ask for more.

Besides, he hasn't given any indication of wanting more even if I wanted to ask.

Co-parents. That's what we are.

That's what we will be.

15
___
DEX

I tried.

I mean, I think I really tried.

Alright, I confess, I may not have tried as hard as I told myself I should, but dammit, I tried not to get involved with Tatum. I told myself to keep things simple, but that is way easier said than done with her. She was great at my place the other night. Down to earth, personable, and funny. She's not the dramatic type, nor is she someone who wants me based on my hockey status.

She's genuinely kind to me but isn't afraid to hold her ground either and I like that about her. I like a lot of things about her.

The other night was a weak moment for me. I gave in to my desires. I allowed myself to taste her again and now she's all I want. And herein lies my conflict.

How do I stay away from the woman who gave me unequivocally the best sex of my life? How do I keep my distance from the woman carrying my child when admittedly, I'm attracted to her?

I need her in my life to help me raise our child, but I don't know how to do relationships. Not in the way she deserves. I've never given a woman as much of me as I've already given Tatum. I don't ask women out on dates. I don't woo them with gifts and flowers and all that girly stuff. It's always been plain and simple with me. A night of sex and orgasms and nothing more.

But with Tatum, I find myself wondering what more might look like. Feel like.

I don't believe two people should be forced together for the sake of their children. My parents were horrible examples of that notion and I won't do that to our child, but at the same time, even the idea of Tatum raising my child with another man...the thought of another man touching her... kissing her. It makes my skin crawl.

"Fuck!"

"What the hell, Foster?" Coach Denovah shouts from the bench. "Defense is supposed to keep the puck away from the net. What is this, your first goddamn day?"

He's right.

I'm not the least bit focused on this practice.

I'm basically phoning it in and I imagine all the guys know it. This is why I love them like brothers though. They're not rubbing it in my face that I'm fucking up left and right. They've all had bad days. But I'm sure I'll be the subject of an intervention when practice is over.

"You want to talk about it?" Hawken murmurs in the shower stall next to me. Of course, the son of a bitch corners me in the shower where I can't run.

"What's there to talk about? I sucked major ass out there today. I just have a lot on my mind."

"Exactly dipshit. That's why I'm asking if you want to talk about it?"

"And what should I say, Hawk? What do you want to know? That I kissed Tatum the other night and it was the second-best kiss of my goddamn life? That I ate her out like a starving man at a fucking all you can eat buffet and it's still not enough?"

"Who's eating who in the what now?" Quinton tosses his towel on the hook and steps into the next stall.

"Not important."

"Except it is important," Hawk says. "Shouldn't we be celebrating this momentous occasion when Dex Foster confirms his dick drought is officially over?"

I shake my head. "My dick had nothing to do with that night. I just..." I bow my head letting the water wash over me. "I couldn't stand it anymore. Being around her all day... I was drawn to her. I wanted to kiss her all evening and then she let me feel the baby kick and I was fucking blown away. Like, for this fleeting moment I could see my life in five to ten years. Snuggled on the couch with my wife and kids. Seeing Tatum in the crowd when I play. I could see it all and it scared me half to death. I tried to end the evening and take her home before I did anything stupid. I really did but she stopped me and she kept apologizing like she had done something wrong and she hadn't done a damn thing wrong, she was just so fucking...perfect and I couldn't stop myself so, I kissed her."

Hawken frowns. "And that's bad because...?"

My emotions burst out of me all at once. "Because I don't know what the fuck I'm doing here! This smoking hot woman who doesn't give two shits what I do for a living is carrying my child and I think I like her. Like, really fucking like her, but I haven't had an honest to God relationship since..." I shake my head. "I don't know. High school? And even then, it was only a month or two. I'm not the relationship guy. I'm not the guy she deserves. I'm the fucking peacock who ruffles his pretty feathers in front of the ladies to get them to take notice, except in place of feathers, I use my dick."

"Sooo...you're just...a cock?" Milo smirks, walking into the showers.

I can't help but huff out a little laugh. "Fuck you, Landric."

Hawk turns his water off and grabs his towel. "Look man, I think you're overthinking this whole thing."

"Agreed." Quinton nods. "Who the hell cares if you've never had a relationship before. If you're attracted to Tatum—for more reasons than just her smoking hot body, your words not mine—and you like her, then let whatever happens happen."

"And if it doesn't work out between the two of you, that doesn't mean your baby is going to be any less loved. You know that. Co-parenting can work if the two of you both put forth the effort."

"Do you want to be with her, Dex?" Milo asks.

I let out a huge sigh as I turn my water off and grab my towel. "I don't want to *not* be with her. I mean right now, I want to be around her every minute of every goddamn day and it kills me when I can't be where she is. I worry about her. I worry about the baby. I want to keep them safe. I want to have control over a situation I have zero control over. But what I know I don't want is for another man to take my place. That will fucking kill me. Or I'll kill him... one or the other."

"Well, I think you've pretty much made up your mind then." Milo grins. "Sounds like you know how you feel. You just have to allow yourself to sit in those feelings. Stop denying yourself the chance to be happy. I know hockey is life, but there's more to life beyond the game and it's okay to want it."

We circle up before hitting the ice for tonight's game, my adrenaline surging through my body. Tonight, is the first time Tatum will get to watch me live and something about that makes me want to play my absolute best.

I want to impress her.

I want to show her how good I am.

That I'm not just a horny single man she met on vacation.

"HUSTLE, HIT, AND NEVER QUIT!" we shout together and then wait for our names to be called. One by one we take the ice and when I hear my name, there's a rush of excitement as the crowd cheers and I take my place along the line up. Immediately I look over to where I know the girls are supposed to be sitting but Charlee and Rory are the only ones there. Carissa is in the tunnel so I know she'll join them later, but where is Tatum?

Bathroom probably.

That explains it.

Following both national anthems, we take our positions for the puck drop and the game is on. I take my first shift along with Nelson, fighting to keep the puck out of our territory and working together to get our team to the other end of the ice. I'm one hundred percent focused, but the very moment I come off the ice, I notice Tatum is once again absent from her seat. I can't get to Rory or Charlee to ask where she is, but I start to worry something is wrong.

"You alright?" Colby asks when he notices my gaze darting around the arena.

"I can't find Tatum. She was supposed to be here tonight."

Colby looking over towards the ladies, his wife now with Charlee and Rory. His brow furrows. "Bathroom? She is pretty pregnant and all."

"Yeah, maybe. And if that's the case, I'll feel terrible for making her have to walk so much to get to the rest room. I should've gotten them a suite."

"Carissa said they wanted to be down front."

"Yeah, I know, I just..." I shake my head. "I don't like that I can't see her."

"Relax man. I'm sure everything is fine. If it wasn't, they would've told you."

That's true.

If there were an emergency, Rory would've told Carissa who would've told Coach and he would call me off the ice. I take a deep breath and try to relax as best I can while staying in the zone so we can pull off another win.

After the first period, we're back in the locker room and I'm throwing my gloves off and reaching for my phone. There's no note from Tatum, but there is one from Rory.

RORY

> FYI – Tate isn't coming tonight. Called and said she was feeling uncomfortable and a little crampy. She didn't want to text you and upset you. 🩶

My shoulders fall and my chest tightens.

She didn't want to upset me?

"Shit."

"She okay?" Hawken asks next to me knowing exactly what I'm worried about.

"Yeah." I shake my head. "I mean she's feeling crampy and shit so she didn't want to come but I feel badly that she was afraid to tell me herself. Rory said she didn't want to upset me. Maybe I put too much pressure on her."

"Nah. You didn't pressure her at all. It was Rory who asked her to come, right?"

"Yeah."

"Then don't sweat it. I'm sure everything is fine. She's super pregnant. I'm sure that's uncomfortable. Cut her some slack."

"Yeah. You're right."

Hawken encourages me not to text her so my mind can stay sharp for the rest of the game. I know he's right. He always has my best interest in mind and he's never steered me wrong. Still, I'm itching to know she's okay.

Second period against Toronto whipped our asses and we're now starting the third period two goals behind. Not an impossibility for us, but fuck, Toronto is playing hard tonight. With two minutes to go, Shay gets possession of the puck and tries to pop it in the net but , it just misses. Malone rebounds with a wraparound but their goalie is fierce and blocks his shot. Toronto dodges two bullets on this shift, and then Nelson and Landric are back on the ice.

I sprint across the ice as Toronto moves the puck into Zeke's territory. Nelson tries to get to it but Shostakopf maneuvers in front of him, takes control, and passes across the ice to Toronto's center who takes a shot. Blocked by Landric's stick. The puck goes into the corner and I chase after it, checking Shostakopf against the glass and swinging the puck to safety. Nelson makes a high arcing pass to Landric who takes his chance moving down the ice, Shay and Malone on his wings and he wraps around the net but passes to Shay just as Toronto's goalie shifts for a wrap-around goal and it's too late! Shay locks in the puck, shoots, and scores!

Any other night, I would be fucking pissed over such a close loss, but tonight I keep my head down and my mouth shut. Toronto played hard and they deserved the win. And now we have shit to push through next week before we face off against the Carolina Storm. Coach doesn't ask me to do press, thank God, so once I complete my post-game routine, and hit the shower, I say goodbye to the guys and head out to check on Tatum.

ME

Hey! I'm sorry you weren't feeling well enough for the game tonight. I'm on my way, can I bring you anything?

ME

Tatum?

ME

You okay?

I don't hear back from her at all during my drive to her apartment, so I step on the gas and pray I'm worrying over nothing. When I get there, I notice her car in her parking spot so I know she's home and when I look up to the second floor, I see her light is on.

Okay. Phew.

Maybe she'll let me give her a foot rub or a massage.

Anything to help her feel better.

But when I get to her door, my Spidey senses tell me something's not right.

Knock, knock, knock.

"Tatum?"

She doesn't answer so I knock a little louder. "Tate? Are you in there?"

"DEX!" she shouts, and not in a good way. Something is wrong. I jiggle the doorknob but the door is locked.

"Tate, the door is locked. Can you let me in?"

"I...I CAAAAAN'T! DEX! HELP ME!"

Oh fuck.

Is she hurt?

What the hell is going on?

Is she okay? The baby?

I pound on the door not giving two shits who I wake up. "TATE! The door is locked," I tell her again, jiggling the fuck out of the doorknob.

Keys idiot!

You have her key!

I grab my keys from my pocket and with a shaky hand, jiggle one into the keyhole but it's not going in.

What the fuck?

Why isn't it working?

"DEX!"

"Shit! Okay, I'M COMING IN TATE!"

With all my weight and brute force, I body check the entire door, breaking the lock and nearly falling as the door swings open. Nothing I can't pay to have fixed later.

"Tatum?" I look around her living room but she's not there. Her television is on, and there's a bowl of uneaten cereal on the coffee table.

Fruit Loops?

"Dex! I'm in the BAAAAATHROOM!"

I'm at the bathroom door in less than three seconds and oh, my God, I am not prepared for what I see next.

Tatum is standing at her bathroom sink, trying to breathe, her hand under her stomach. A puddle of...fuck, I don't know what that is...is on the floor beneath her.

"Tatum? What—"

"My water broke, Dex!" she cries. "And this baby is coming right fucking now!"

O *ooh shit.*
I swallow my sudden nerves and try to assess the situation but fuck if I know what the hell I'm doing. "Uh, okay, babe. Don't panic. Everything's going to be fine. I can carry you to the car and we'll—"

"AAAHHHHHH!" She grabs her stomach and doubles over, her face contorted in pain. She shakes her head. "No cars. Now Dex!" She's holding her breath as she shouts. "This little fucker is coming right NOW!"

Shiiiiiiiit.

Fuck!

Oh, shit!

What the fuck do I do?

I stare at a sweaty, teary-eyed, slightly panicking Tatum, completely dumbfounded as to what I should be doing right now, inwardly panicking myself, but trying to not let her see my emotions.

"Okay. Okay." I nod for no other reason than to reassure myself. "Alright, we can do this. Let me call 9-1-1 and they'll be here before we ca—Whoa! What are you doing?"

I watch in horror as she jimmies her soaked panties down her legs and kicks them off and then tries to lower herself to the floor. I'm at her side in an instant helping her.

"Fuck! Tatum! You mean right fucking now?" Oh, my God, I didn't think she was that serious!

"I need to push, Dex! I feel it coming. Please help me! You need to deliver this baby!"

I throw my hands up in defense. "Whoa! Babe. I don't..." I shake my head. "I can't...I have no idea—"

She grabs my arm and growls like I've never heard her before, LISTEN UP SPERM DONOR! I DID NOT CARRY YOUR LITTLE SWIMMER THIS LONG FOR YOU TO WALTZ INTO MY LIFE AT THE END OF THIS PREGNANCY AND NOT HELP ME WHEN THE GOING GETS TOUGH AND RIGHT NOW IT'S HELLA-TOUGH AND FUCKING SCARY, DO YOU GET THAT? HUH? DO YOU GET THAT A SMALL SCREAMING MONSTER IS ABOUT TO BE PUSHED THROUGH PARTS OF ME THAT ENJOYED YOUR PRETTY PIERCED DICK EIGHT MONTHS AGO?"

"Yeah...yeah, babe. I get it."

"THEN PUSSY UP AND GET THE FUCK DOWN HERE RIGHT NOW AND CATCH THE ONE I FAILED TO SWALLOW YOU SON OF A BITCH!" I've never seen a demon possessed woman before except for maybe *Ghostbusters*, or *The Exorcist*, but if demon possession is real, I think I'm seeing it right now for the very first time.

I'm nodding without saying any words and grabbing towels off the shelf in her bathroom to help prepare. I roll a few towels together and place them behind Tatum's head and then lay several over the puddle on her floor between her legs.

"I-I-I-don't know what to do, Tatum, but I'm here, okay? I'm fucking here. I'll catch the baby. Whatever you need." I'm squatting down between her legs as if I'm about to catch a football. "God, please don't be too slippery. Do not drop this baby. Why haven't I been carrying grip gloves for the past month?" I shake my head. "No, I've got this. I can do it."

"Dex!"

My head snaps up. "What?"

"Call 9-1-1 and tell them I'm having a fucking baby!"

"Right. Yes. Okay."

"AAAAAHHHHHHHHHH!"

Oh, God.

Oh, God.

She's screaming.

This is happening.

With shaky hands, I grab my phone from my pocket and push the appropriate buttons for the 9-1-1 operator.

"9-1-1. What is your emergency?"

Above Tate's screams I shout into my phone, "She's having a fucking baby right here in her bathroom. Send help!"

"Okay Sir. Where are you located?"

"Belford apartment complex in Archer Heights. Apartment eight!"

"AHHHHHHHHHHHHHHHHH   DEX   IT'S

COMING!" she screams. "OH SHIT, IT HURTS! IT HURTS!"

"I know, baby. I'm right here, okay? Oh...God. Is that? Oh...ew...God...Fucking hell!"

"DEX!"

"You're doing great. They're going to send someone." I squeeze my eyes closed and shout, "Please God, send someone!"

"An ambulance is on its way, Sir, but don't hang up. I'm going to talk you through this."

"IT'S COMING! SOMETHING'S HAPPENING! DEX I HAVE TO PUUUUUSH!"

She bears down, her face scrunching as she pushes with all her might. Her legs are spread wide in front of me and oh, my God!

"The baby's head! I see it! It's coming!" I shout into the phone.

"Okay, Sir, do you have some clean cloth or towels around you?"

"Y-y-yes! Towels! I have towels! Oh God this is...this is bloody! And shit...what is that?"

"AHHHHHHHHHHHHHHHH DEEEEEX"

She pushes again and I watch in both horror and amazement as our child slides out with ease. "Tatum, it's our baby! You're doing it! It's almost out!"

The lady on the phone says to me, "Don't pull on anything, Sir, alright? Let Mama do her thing. Is everyone doing okay so far?"

"Uhh..." I glance up at Tatum and my heart breaks for her. She looks like she's in more pain than any hockey injury could ever give me. She's a sweaty mess and the fear and panic in her eyes is enough to make me want to stop the world from turning so she can get through this ordeal in peace. "There's a lot of umm...fluid...some blood, and the baby looks..."

Good God.

Fuck. My eyes are wet.

I think I'm crying.

"It's beautiful."

"DEX!"

With one hand on my child and the other on Tatum's leg, I squeeze ever so slightly to encourage her to keep going. "You can do this, Tate. One more and it's out. One more little push, okay?"

She nods with a long painful groan and then pushes once more, causing the baby to slide all the way out and into my waiting hands.

"I've got it! I've got it! I've got it!!"

"Great job," the operator says. "Is the baby crying, Sir?"

Panting, Tatum looks on with a smile that quickly falters. "Dex, why isn't it crying?"

"Sir, I want you to put the baby on Mom's chest, okay? Mom, I want you to rub the baby's back."

Tatum lies back on her towels and I place the baby, still connected to her, on her chest, both of us rubbing its back, its legs, and its arms. It feels like minutes go by but I'm sure it's only seconds before the baby starts crying and the both of us release huge sighs of relief. Tatum starts to sob and I would be lying if I said I wasn't crying right along with her.

"There's that beautiful sound. Great job, Mom and Dad," the operator tells us. "As long as Mom and baby are okay, let's make sure baby is warm and covered with a towel or blanket or shirt and your ambulance is just a few minutes away. I'm going to stay on the line until they get there, okay?"

"Thank you. Yes. That's great. Thank you." I hastily pull off my shirt and cover our baby, wanting to keep it as warm as possible.

"You guys did great. Is this your first child?"

"Yes," we both say.

"Well, this will be a great story for you to tell one day. Did you have a little boy or a little girl?"

"Oh fuck, I forgot to look." I glance at Tatum who slowly lifts the baby up so she can see and beams back at me with more tears flowing down her cheeks.

"It's a girl, Dex. We had a girl."

The operator congratulates us once again and my emotions are all over the place.

A girl.

I'm a dad.

To a little girl.

Holy fuck. I'm a dad.

Tatum.

My eyes land on her serene face as she coos calmly to our baby in her arms and I don't think I've ever seen a more beautiful thing. I lean over and kiss our newborn daughter's head and then kiss Tatum's forehead.

"I'm so damn proud of you, Tate. Look at you. You did it."

"We did it," she says, but I shake my head.

"No. Babe, you did this. You did it all and I...I never thought I would ever want to be a dad, but...God. Thank you." Tears slip down my cheeks because fuck it. I can't keep my emotions in check. "Thank you for this."

Hearing the EMS crew near the front door, I call for them so they know where we are and then I step back so they can do their thing.

Taking care of my girls.

My girls.

Tatum and, "My little Tater Tot."

17

TATUM

I t's the middle of the night or early in the morning, when I open my eyes after finally succumbing to the events of the day. Our baby was born at 10:23 PM this evening thanks to the help of the man currently holding her.

My daughter.

Our daughter.

As I open my eyes, I hear his voice singing softly, so I turn my head and spot him stretched out on the small couch in my hospital room. Bent at the knee, because he can't actually stretch his whole self out on the small-scale furniture, he has a baby blanket draped over his lap and cradles our baby in front of him. He softly rubs his large hand over her head and then down the front of her as he whispers to her.

"You are so beautiful; do you know that?" he asks her. "Yes, you are. You look just like your mommy. And one day I'm probably going to want to kill any man who dares to look at you, but right now, *I* can't stop looking at you. I can't believe I'm your daddy, baby girl. I may not be perfect and I'm sure I'm going to make about a gazillion mistakes, but I promise you I will do everything in my power to make sure you and your mommy have a happy life. We'll watch so much hockey together and when you're older I'll teach you how to skate. God, I love you so much already."

Watching him with her. How gentle he is…it brings a smile to my face and a joy to my heart. I can tell he really does love her.

"You know, she probably needs a name," I finally murmur. His head snaps to me, surprised to see me awake.

"Heyyyy," he coos. "Did I wake you? I'm sorry. We were just…" He looks down at our daughter and smiles. "We were just chatting."

"No, you didn't. Hospital beds aren't the most comfortable thing in the world."

"I can get you some extra pillows. Blankets? Are you cold?"

I shake my head, still a bit drowsy. "No. I'm okay. Thank you."

He's quiet for a minute before he speaks again. "How about Summer?"

"What about summer?"

"Her name. Summer."

"It's pretty. What made you think of that?"

He glances at the baby again, swiping a finger over her forehead and smiling down at her. "I don't know. We met in the summer. Summer's a relaxing time for me, for you too given your job. Summer is usually a happy time for a lot of people."

"I like it," I tell him. "Summer Grace? Grace is my

middle name. I was kind of hoping it could be her middle name too."

"Yeah." He nods. "Summer Grace Lowe." I like it.

"No, silly. She would be Summer Grace Foster."

His smile falters. "It would?"

"Is that not okay? You're her father after all. Kids usually take their paternal surnames."

"You...you want her to be a Foster?"

I tilt my head against my pillow. "Of course. You're her dad, Dex."

He whispers her name. "Summer Grace Foster...yeah. I think I love it. It's perfect." He turns to me. "Can she still be my little tater tot?"

His nickname makes me chuckle. "Of course. Always."

He lifts Summer in his arms and brings his lips to her forehead. "You are the most perfect child that has ever been created and I am so fucking proud to be your daddy."

"Have you been holding her and talking to her this whole time?"

"Hell yeah. You need to sleep way more than I do. This is the least I can do."

"You know there's a basinet in here for a reason, right? You can put her in there and get some sleep yourself."

"Not a fucking chance. I'm not leaving her in that plastic box when I can keep her right here next to me. She's safe and warm, right here." He turns and rises from the couch with Summer still in his arms. "I mean, unless you want to hold her."

"I do, but..." I yawn. "I don't want anything to happen to her if I fall back asleep and that seems very likely as my eyes are already feeling heavy again."

Dex leans down so I can kiss our baby and then he kisses the top of my head. I close my eyes and linger in the feel of his lips on me. The warmth of him. Knowing I'm safe and cared for when he's here.

I'm so glad he's here.

"Dex?"

"Yeah, babe?"

I feel myself start to drift back to sleep. "Thank you for doing this with me. For not leaving me alone."

"Tatum, there is nowhere else I would rather be. I promise I'm not going anywhere. Sleep now." He kisses me one last time. "I'll be here when you wake up."

"Dude, it's so my turn. Hand her over."

"No fair, you've already gotten to hold her twice."

"Fuck you, asshat. She's basically my niece."

"Yeah, well she is my niece, dumbass. And don't say fuck in front of the baby. She has ears."

"Yeah, Hawken. Don't say fuck. She's just a baby."

Suddenly all of the guys and Rory breathe in at the same time, their faces frowning.

"Oh, damn," Quinton says. "What's that smell?"

Quinton waves his hand in front of his face. "Woof. That's worse than a day-old gym bag."

Milo nods. "That's worse than all our socks after not washing them throughout playoffs."

"That smells like a shit took a shit," Hawken says. "And then mixed it with someone else's shit."

Rory cocks her head. "How do you even know what that would smell like?"

"Excuse me, you bunch of pussies," Zeke takes Summer from Hawken and cradles her in his big sturdy arms. "But I believe that is the smell of a perfectly ripe newborn baby shit."

"Hey, watch who you're callin' a pussy," Dex narrows his eyes as he takes Summer from Zeke and then gestures to me. "My girl's pussy performed more magic than I have ever fucking seen when she birthed this perfect little gem." He kisses Summer's nose. "She is one bad ass woman. Ain't nothin' weak about a pussy."

"Thank you for telling everyone in the room about my vagina, Dex. I'm sure it's exactly what they wanted to hear."

In all honesty, Dex's compliment almost makes me swoon. Well, that and he refers to me as his girl.

Am I really his girl?

Does he see me that way?

As Dex places Summer in her bassinet to change her diaper, the guys continue their friendly argument.

"You guys, you know I already hold the favorite uncle title, right?"

The guys all stare at Milo. Quinton rolls his eyes.

"Says who?"

"Says my sister. Her kids adore me. I have experience."

Colby laughs. "Her kids put makeup on you and do your nails like a pretty little girl. We've all seen the pictures."

"And duh, that's why I'm the favorite uncle. You just

wait. One day this little princess right here is going to ask to paint your nails and not one of you is going to say no."

"Damn right," Dex tells them. "First one of you to say no to my kid gets a punch to the nuts. No cup allowed."

I snicker. "Dex!"

"What?" He shrugs. "Just doin' my fatherly duties. If my kid says jump, they better ask how high. If my baby says she wants a pony, these guys better be buying her a fuckin' Clydesdale."

Colby finally steps up and takes Summer into his arms once she has a fresh diaper. "Summer Grace, if you ask Uncle Colby for a pony, I'll buy you the whole horse farm. How does that sound?"

Milo rolls his eyes. "Overachiever."

After a couple days of family visits, the introduction between my parents and Dex—they loved him by the way —and visits from the team as well as teacher friends from work, Summer and I were finally being discharged to go home. My mom is staying with me this week to help out with the baby and as grateful as I am for her love and support, I'm nervous about how this is going to work where Dex is concerned.

Dex and I didn't talk about this ahead of time. Perhaps that's my fault. I made all these plans before he showed up in my life but I certainly don't want to push him away. He has as much of a right to Summer as I do, and he wants to be a dad. He wants the midnight feedings and the diaper changes. He wants the bath and bedtime routine. According to him he wants it all.

I only wish I knew, for sure, what *all* means.

Does *all* include me?

Us?

Will we be a family?

Does he want that?

Do I want that?

He's a very high-profile athlete with a rigorous schedule on and off the ice. I know that's where his focus needs to be and I wouldn't blame him for wanting his private time, what little of it he gets.

"Welcome home!" My mom stands just inside my apartment as Dex carries Summer in her car carrier and our duffle bags through the door. "There's my little angel," she coos. "How was the ride?"

I chuckle behind Dex. "I don't think he's ever driven so slowly in my life."

Dex places Summer down on the table and turns. "Can't trust those crazy drivers out there, you know? Besides, the roads could've been icy and I'm not taking any chances."

"Well, thank you for getting my girls home in one piece," Mom says, already unhooking and lifting Summer from her seat.

"Yes, thank you, Dex."

"Of course. Don't mention it."

"God, I could use a shower."

Dex eyes me seriously. "Do you need some help? Even just an arm to steady you? Someone to wash your hair?"

Why is he so sweet and swoony?

"I think I can manage. I just want to wash off the hospital ick and get out of these sexy hospital panties."

"I packed that squirt bottle thing for you. It's in your toiletry bag. The nurse said...well, you know. It would come in handy."

"My super cooch-soaker three thousand?" I wink at Dex who chuckles when I use his name for the all-mighty peri bottle from my hospital bathroom.

"Yeah, that."

"Thank you. It'll come in very handy for the next few days or weeks or...however long this mess takes to go away."

He fidgets a little as Mom makes silly faces at Summer in that way all grandparents do.

"Alright, umm, well, why don't I run out and get us all some dinner? It'll be good for you to eat some real food."

"That sounds fabulous. I'm starving."

"I'll get anything you want. Name it."

"Oh, umm, Ooooh!" My eyes grow. "What about mac and cheese from Freda's Diner? And maybe a few salads? Oh, and their meatballs. Oh, my God I feel like I could eat a ton of those right now."

"Freda's it is." He leans over and kisses my temple. "Relax in the shower and I'll take care of dinner while your mom has some baby time. Text me if you need anything else, okay?"

"Thank you, Dex."

"See you soon."

18

DEX

I called ahead to place an order with Freda's Diner and then stopped at the closest Meijer to pick up some of Tatum's favorites. Orange juice, goldfish crackers, her favorite tea, a bag of Hershey kisses, yogurt, and several restaurant gift cards she can use to order meals while I'm out of town. Not that her mother can't cook for her, but this puts my mind at ease knowing she should eat well while I'm gone.

I'm beginning to hate that I'll be gone.

Fucking hockey.

With my arms full of groceries and dinner, I open Tatum's door to find her breastfeeding Summer on the couch while her mom cleans a few dishes in the sink. Watching Tatum breastfeed is nothing I haven't seen before in the past couple days but being here...it feels like I'm invading her privacy. I give her a soft smile and then retreat to the kitchen to put away groceries and plate some dinner for her.

Once she's done feeding, I make sure Tatum gets to eat

while I hold our daughter. I soak her in as much as I can, her sweet scent, the sound of her breathing, the feel of her little warm body against my chest, the feel of her whole hand wrapped around just one of my fingers, the way my entire soul calms when she's in my arms. She's a whole new piece of heaven I never realized could exist for me.

Shortly after dinner and her feeding, Tatum and I work together to give Summer a light sponge bath, my hand cradling her tiny body while Tate sprinkles warm water over her. Her little eyes close as if she's enjoying a relaxing spa treatment and it makes us both smile. Tatum's mom watches on, snapping several pictures on her phone. I'll be glad to have those pictures. A memory of a happy moment together with my tater tot and the woman who changed me from the king of one-night stands, to someone I never expected to be.

A dad.

Tatum lets me put Summer to sleep, so I spend a few minutes singing to her and whispering as many affirmations as I can come up with so she always remembers how much I believe in her. Once she's out, I lay her down in her crib and step out of her room, a little unsure of what to do next. This entire situation is awkward. Partly because Tatum's mom is here with us and I have no idea what she's told her about us.

Does she think we're together?

Does she know we're not really together?

Should I stay?

Should I go?

The very thought of walking out Tatum's door and leaving her and Summer here without me makes me physically ill. But on the other hand, I wasn't invited to stay, nor have we talked about what might happen once they were discharged from the hospital. I have this deep sense of dread that this whole thing is going to be very bad for me, but what choice do I have? Tatum hasn't said she wants me here and I have to respect that.

"Mom, I can get you some blankets and a pillow," I hear Tatum say when I walk back to the living room.

"Don't worry yourself, Tate. I know where they are in your hall closet."

Since I'm standing right next to the aforementioned closet, I open it and pull out two blankets and a pillow from the top shelf, carrying them to Mrs. Lowe.

"Oh, thank you, Dex. I appreciate that."

"Sure thing." I hand her the blankets and then rub my hands down my sides and catch Tatum's eyes. "I guess I'll uh, leave you two alone for the night then...if there's nothing else you need?"

"Oh. Uh..." Her brows pinch and she glances toward her mother as she steps up toward me. "Right. Uh, I'm sorry."

She didn't ask me to stay before we got here. It wasn't in the plan, not that we had a plan to begin with. I sweep her hair back, cupping her face in my hand.

"You have nothing to be sorry for, Tatum. You need your rest and I um, I have to be at the arena for morning workout anyway."

That's a lie.

Or an excuse.

Whichever.

Her shoulders fall and dammit I want to scoop her up

and carry her to bed and hold her all night. The mother of my child. She's fucking Wonder Woman and I want to make sure she knows that. How much I appreciate her. How amazing of a human I think she is.

"Oh. Okay."

I smooth a hand down her shoulder. "But I'll stop in before practice, to check on Summer and make sure you don't need anything, alright?"

"Dex, you don't have to d—"

"I want to, Tatum." I cup her face in my hands gently, my fingers playing with a few strands of her hair. "I'll make you breakfast. You have to eat. For you and the baby."

She smiles. "I know."

I say goodbye to Tatum's mother and then turn to leave, but Tatum catches my hand with hers when I turn for the door. "Dex?"

"Yeah?"

She squeezes my hand. "Thank you. For everything."

Fuck I hate that I'm leaving.

Why can't I be man enough to tell her I'm staying?

Why didn't she just ask me to stay?

I wouldn't turn her down.

Not knowing what to say because why the hell is she thanking me when I feel like I should be constantly thanking her, I squeeze my eyes closed and kiss her forehead, lingering there longer than I know I should because fuck, I can't tear myself away.

"I'll see you tomorrow."

And then I walk out the door, leaving Tatum and my newborn daughter to spend their first night at home together.

Without me.

"I didn't expect to see you tonight," Rory states when I step inside our condo and find her working on lesson plans at the table.

Sulking into one of the chairs across from her, I release an overexaggerated sigh. Partly because I'm exhausted, but also because I'm...fucking sad.

"Believe me, I didn't want to be here tonight. At least not like this."

Rory cringes. "What happened? Is everything okay?"

"Everything is fine," I mumble. "Summer is great. Tatum is exhausted but she's a fucking trooper."

"So why are you here and not there?"

"Because I wasn't invited to stay there."

"Since when has that stopped you?"

"Since we're not in a relationship, Ror. We're not... sleeping together and her mom is there with her. I have no idea what Tatum may or may not have told her about me and us and it felt awkward as fuck once I put the baby to sleep. I did what I thought was best and left...even though it's killing me to be away from her."

"Her who?" Rory's brow lifts and she grins at me.

"Summer Grace, of course."

"Ah." She nods. "Okay. For a moment there I thought maybe you were talking about Tate."

My jaw ticks as I watch her expression change. Like she's challenging me to deny my feelings for Tatum.

"Okay, yeah. Tatum too." I avert my eyes from my sister, shaking my head. "I like her."

Rory scoffs out a laugh. "Tell me something I don't already know."

"I mean, like her, like her, Ror."

She feigns shock and surprise, bringing her hand up to her mouth. "Bring me a sweater. I think Hell must be freezing over."

"What?"

Her head snaps to the windows. "Did you see those pigs flying around earlier? I swear there were so many—"

"Rory," I deadpan.

"I mean, am I in some kind of alternate universe where my brother sleeps with women more than once and actually has relationships with them?"

"Alright, alright, smartass."

Her eyes grow huge. "Oh. EM. GEE, DEX! What if you have lots of little baby Dex's all over the country from your past sexscapades? What if other women have gotten pregnant and just not told you?"

I'm pretty sure all the blood drains from my body in this very moment as the thought of my fathering multiple children with multiple mothers makes me immediately sick to my stomach and I very nearly vomit.

"Whoa! I didn't really mean it, Dex."

"Rory!"

I like Tatum too much for that to happen. The possibility of having to ever tell her I have other children out there shatters my nerves. "I can't hurt Tatum like that, Ror." I shake my head. "I won't. Fucking Christ, that would be my worst nightmare."

"Relax, Brother." She pats my frigid hand. "Is Tatum the only woman you've slept with who didn't know who you were?"

"Yeah. I'm ninety-nine percent sure."

"Then I'm certain you have nothing to worry about. Any other woman in that predicament would've come forward by now because they would've wanted fame or money." She bobs her head. "Or both."

"Tell me what to do, Rory."

"What do you mean?"

"It's my baby girl's first night at home and I'm not fucking there and it's killing me. I want her here. I want Tatum here." I rest my elbows on the table, my head in my hands. "While we were in the hospital, we were this little, tiny family. Just the three of us in this bubble of fucking perfection. And the whole time it felt...right. I could see it all. I could see Tatum holding our baby while I was on the ice. I could see them cheering for the team. I could see me celebrating with her. I could see me putting Summer to sleep and then taking care of Tatum. I wanted that feeling to be real."

"It can be real."

"How?" I jerk my arms out in frustration. "How can it be real when I wasn't even invited to stay with her tonight? She doesn't want me there, Rory."

"You don't know that, Dex. Maybe she's scared."

"Of what?"

"Of..." she shrugs. "I don't know. This is yet another new thing for her this year. Motherhood. Being a responsible parent. She has more than just herself to think about now."

"And I can't help her with that when she's there and I'm here."

"Soooo get rid of the roadblock."

"The what?"

"The roadblock. Nut up and tell her how you feel, Dex. Make a nursery here for Summer. Show Tate you have space for her here. Invite her here. It's not like we don't have the room."

"You would be okay with that?"

"Are you kidding me?" she squeals. "Baby time anytime I want? Hell yes, I'm okay with it. And we could ride to work together. I could babysit while you...you know, woo her and shit."

"How do I do that? The...wooing?"

"Acknowledge her. Romance her. Take her out on dates. Make sure she feels appreciated and loved and desired. I promise if you can do all those things, she may just be the best thing to ever happen to you."

Pretty damn sure she is the best damn thing to ever happen to me.

"Do you think you might be willing to help me with a slight redecoration project? I mean I know it'll take a little time to put together but I wouldn't mind getting your decorating help. You're good at that stuff."

The beaming smile on her face is all I need to know her answer, but she gives me a resounding, "Absolutely!" anyway.

Using the key she gave me to her apartment, I let myself in around five in the morning and hear Summer crying in her room.

Yes!

Daddy's coming, tater tot!

But when I step into the doorway of her room, Tatum is already up.

"Hey," I whisper, smiling at my favorite ladies. "How are my girls this morning?"

Tatum yawns. "Tired. This little one was a bit fussy last night."

She wasn't the only one.

Must run in the family.

"Has she eaten?"

Tatum nods. "I just fed her about fifteen minutes ago. She must have some gas."

"Why don't you let me handle it while you go back to sleep. Then I'll make you some breakfast, alright?"

"You sure?"

"Absolutely." I reach out my arms to lift Summer from Tatum's arms. "Daddy's here, tater tot. Let's let Mommy get some more rest, okay?" I kiss her sweet face several times and then hold her against my shoulder, patting her back. "Does my little girl have a tummy ache?"

Her quiet little cries are adorable. It's almost as if she can understand me.

"You sure you're okay with her?"

I inhale a deep breath as I sway back and forth continuing to pat Summer's back to help relieve her of her gas. "I'm exactly where I want to be, Tate. I promise I've got this."

She smiles at the two of us, Summer and me. "I know you do. I'm glad you're here. We missed you last night."

I fucking missed you too.

Tatum retreats back to her bedroom and I sit in the glider happy to have my girl in my arms.

"Did you miss Daddy last night, tater tot?" I murmur to her as her crying settles. "Because I missed you like crazy. Daddy didn't sleep much last night either because I wanted to be where you were. You've been such a cuddle bug these past few days and I fucking missed that. And don't tell your mommy this, but I really missed her to."

We sit in silence together for several minutes. Summer falling back asleep, me gliding back and forth in the chair so she's in a constant state of soothing motion.

"I think I really like your mom, Summer Grace," I whisper against her, my hand slowly rubbing across her tiny back. "She was all I thought about most of the summer. It's like she was lost to me and then I found her again only now things are very different and I don't know what to do about that."

Though I'm pretty sure she's asleep, I keep talking to her anyway. It's not like I have anyone else to talk to. "You think you can put in a good word for me? Maybe tell your mom I'm a good guy? I mean I know I've had my wild moments, but there's nothing I wouldn't do for you, Tater Tot. And nothing I wouldn't do to make your mom happy."

I close my eyes for a good twenty minutes or so, Summer peacefully sleeping in my arms. Somewhere in the late six o'clock hour, I finally stand and place the baby in her crib and then head to the kitchen to make breakfast for Tatum. I pour her a glass of orange juice but keep it in the fridge to stay cold and make a pot of coffee so it's ready for her. Then I grab the ingredients to make us all omelets and pop a few pieces of toast in the toaster.

"You really know your way around a kitchen." Mrs. Lowe stands in the doorway watching me.

"Good morning Mrs. Lowe. I'm sorry, I didn't mean to wake you. Just wanted to get breakfast started before I have to be at practice."

"You didn't. I promise. I'm used to being up early. Well, that and the coffee smells good." She smiles at me. "And please, call me Theresa. Mrs. Lowe is my mother-in-law and just between us, she's a fucking piece of work."

Her words make me laugh, but I make sure to do so as quietly as possible. "Oh, well, that sounds like a story and a half."

She hums. "Yep. And I would need a day and a half to tell it. Trust me. So how did you become such a master in the kitchen?"

I scoff softly. "I would probably need a good day and a half to tell you all that too, but let's just say I didn't uh...I didn't have quite the upbringing that Tatum was blessed with, from what she's told me."

Theresa nods. "She is pretty close with her siblings. I guess we were pretty lucky that way. Is Rory your only sibling?"

"Yes. And you could say I sort of raised her...raised us both from about fifteen on."

"Oh, I'm so sorry."

I shrug off the pity. "It is what it is. She needed me and I needed...someone. Anyone, I guess, back then, so I made sure she was taken care of. Dad was nowhere to be seen and our mother..." I sigh as I flip an omelet over in the pan. "She enjoyed drugs and alcohol more than she enjoyed being a mom."

"If you don't mind my asking, how did you get into hockey with all that responsibility?"

"Oh, we weren't a poor family. My parents both had money. Mom got half of Dad's when he left and that coupled with her own salary was enough to...shall we say keep her kids busy and away from the house for hours at a time?"

"That must've been hard."

"At times, yes. Others, it was an escape. Like I said, it is what it is and now this is where I am."

She pours herself a cup of coffee, nodding silently. Feeling me out, I'm sure.

"So, you met Tatum in Key West, huh?"

I snort a laugh as I remember that day so clearly. I'll spare her mom the kinky details.

"I did, yeah. My teammate was getting married down there and the uh..." I clear my throat. "The friend she was there with actually encouraged me to talk to Tatum."

I steal a glance her way and Theresa is smirking at me as she listens. "Of course, she did. That Eliza is a sneaky friend sometimes."

"But I need you to know this thing we have going on now..."

"A baby..."

"Right. The baby. This isn't something I take lightly. I'll be here one hundred and ten percent for Tatum and Summer. They're important to me. Both of them. They'll want for nothing. I'll make sure of it."

"And what if she wants you?"

My head snaps up from glancing back down at my pan. "What?"

There's that knowing smirk again. "I asked what if she wants you? Are you prepared for that?"

"I..."

Is her mom really asking me this?

Does she know something I don't know?

"How many one-night stands did you have on that vacation, Dex?"

My cheeks heat at her question. "Just...uh...just the one."

God that's embarrassing to admit to my one-night stand's mother.

"And how many had you had before meeting my daughter?"

My eyes grow huge and my ass clenches because fuck me, Tatum's mom is seriously asking me how many women I've slept with. As if I keep track.

Swallowing my pride because I want to be as honest and open with her as possible so she knows I'm genuine, I answer her. "Uh, Theresa, I'm not the kind of guy who keeps track, so I don't have a number to give you if that's what you're asking for, but if I'm being completely honest, that number is probably higher than it is lower."

"Uh huh."

My shoulders fall. "Look, I know you have no reason to think I'm a decent guy. Yes, I've slept with several women in my day. They hang on us after games when we're out. It's offered up all the time, so yes, I've... taken advantage a few times."

"A few times." She smiles.

"But then I met Tatum. And she was...different."

Theresa's eyes narrow. "How so?"

Well Mom, she stuck her finger in my ass and brought me to orgasm faster than anyone ever has and I haven't forgotten.

"She had no idea who I was."

"Yes, that sounds like my Tatum." She chuckles softly. "She was never one to pay attention to a lot of sports unless her brothers were around hogging the television."

"It was a refreshing change to meet someone who wanted to talk to me. Just me. Not hockey player me. Not celebrity me. Not millionaire me. Just...me." I shake my head. "I'd never had anyone treat me like that before."

"You know she's divorced?"

"Yeah. She told me."

"That was a horrific time for her. She's resilient and strong but walking in on her husband and best friend being unfaithful hurt her a lot."

"I can only imagine."

"Have you ever been in a relationship before, Dex?"

"Are you asking me if I've ever cheated?"

"Yes."

"No. Not all men are douchebags. Some of us are decent men."

Unless we're talking about the things I did with your daughter in the bedroom because that was anything but decent.

"So once again I'll say, you want to be in your daughter's life, but what if my daughter wants you to be in her life too?"

"Then I'm all in."

Her brows raise. "Just like that?"

"Just like that."

"You're sure?"

I plate her an omelet and slide the plate in front of her. "Theresa, if Tatum wants me in her life, she has me. One hundred percent. I would do anything for her."

"And only her?"

I pull out the chair opposite her and take a seat, making sure she sees how serious I am right now. "If this helps me pass this interview I seem to be having right now, I'll tell you this. I haven't slept with anyone in ages. Certainly not since Tatum walked back into my life unexpectedly, and she's all I thought about all summer long. If we would've shared contact info back then, I assure you I would've been in touch."

A genuine smile spreads across her face. "You're good for her Dex. You did a wonderful job delivering Summer and taking care of Tatum at the hospital. And I have a strong feeling you'll continue to do the same now that she's home. You keep playing your cards right, and you just might be the best thing to ever happen to her."

"That's the second time I've heard that in the last twenty-four hours. You must've been talking to my sister."

Theresa laughs. "Nope. But now that I know that I can't wait to officially meet her."

So, she's giving me the go-ahead with Tatum, but she's not giving me any indication of Tatum's feelings one way or the other.

Why are relationships so overwhelmingly confusing?

19

TATUM

Knock, knock, knock!

"Hmm, what do you think it'll be this time?" I ask Rory as I hop off the couch next to where she snuggles a sleeping Summer. Every day this week, there has been a gift delivered here from Dex who is playing a string of six away-games. First it was a mega bouquet of roses along with an oversized soft blanket and my favorite tea along with a musical snow globe for Summer's room. Then it was a larger than I would ever need smart television with a full cable package complete with any possible sports channel I might need to watch the Red Tails play. Then he sent a complete home spa basket with warming slippers, a soft robe, and all the smelly-good bath and shower things I could ever want and a rubber duckie blow-up bathtub filled with baby gifts for Summer.

"After the last delivery of every hockey romance book he could find on Amazon, I'm not sure what he could possibly come up with." Rory chuckles softly. She's been so

208

great about staying with me or checking in on me and Summer while Dex is away. Having my mom here for the first week was great too, but even then, I was ready for her to go back home and let me get my feet wet doing this whole parenting thing on my own.

"And don't forget the small library of baby books he sent for Summer too," I giggle. "How many daddy/daughter books are even out there in the world?"

"Oh God," Rory says. "Don't ask him that. He'll consider it a challenge to find every single one!"

I answer the door to find the same delivery woman who has been showing up here every day this week smiling at me. Charlee was here with me the other day and let her in on why all these gifts have been delivered and now she's my number one fan.

She shakes her head. "Miss Lowe, I'm beginning to think someone really has a crush on you and I'm a little invested now in how this is all going to work out. Do you have a social media platform I should follow to keep myself updated?"

Laughing, I too, shake my head. "No, I'm sorry. I don't really do social media, but if I had to guess, at the rate these packages keep showing up, you'll be here for the next couple days at least."

"I look forward to it!" she says. "Here's today's box. But this one is addressed to Summer Grace Foster."

"Thank you so much." I take the box from her, shaking my head in disbelief. "Oh, my gosh, I can't wait to see what he did."

"You're very welcome. Have a great day, Ms. Lowe."

"Thank you. You too!"

SUSAN RENEE

I shut the door and carry the box over to the coffee table in front of Rory.

"Awww, he sent something just for her?"

"Looks like it."

"Just when I wondered if my brother had it in him to be cute and sincere, he goes and does shit like this."

I bite my bottom lip to keep from smiling too hard because I would be lying if I said I wasn't loving the fact that he's remembering us in some way while he can't be here. It's wonderful to get a few texts from him every night and usually a call throughout the day if he isn't too busy but knowing he's going the extra mile to make me smile every day...yeah. That isn't a bad thing.

With the help of a pair of scissors nearby, I open the large box and pull out yet another basket filled with diapers, wipes, and a bunch of hockey themed onesies in a multitude of colors.

"Oh, my God! Look at these!" I pull out the onesies and open one that reads

Hockey Baby! Yep. I arrived with missing teeth.

Another one says

Daddy's little hockey princess.

And there's even one that says

Proof Daddy can score.

"How adorable!" I squeal. "I can't wait to put one of these on her and send him a pic tonight. He'll lose his shit."

"He totally will." Rory laughs. "God, this little princess has her daddy wrapped around her finger."

"That she does."

"Like mother like daughter, huh?"

"What do you mean?"

Rory cocks her head. "What I mean is I'm pretty damn sure you have my brother wrapped around your finger as well."

"Oh, I don't know if I would say that."

She huffs out a laugh. "Well then you're totally blind."

My smile falters and I sink into my oversized chair staring blankly at my friend.

"Tatum, in all the years I've known my brother, he's always been the player. The guy who walks into a bar after a game, picks up a woman, and leaves just like that."

The thought makes my stomach turn.

"But then you happened and I don't know that he's been with another woman since. You are all he talked about all summer. His mystery girl: the one who blew his mind. The one who caused him to take up knitting because his mind was so distracted, he needed something to focus on." She laughs. "And then you're pregnant with his kid and his world is flipped upside down yet he doesn't run. Tate, I've never seen him like this. Ever. He has feelings for you. You have to see that. It's killing him that he's not here with you. With Summer." She gestures to the gifts sitting around my living room. "He's never done anything even remotely close to this. For anyone. Not even me."

I fiddle with my pajama pants, rubbing the material

between my thumb and forefinger, an anxious habit. "Can I ask you something, Rory?"

"Of course."

"Would you think I was crazy if I told you I might love him?"

A sincere smile spreads across her face. "Only because he's my brother and I used to put up with him farting in my face and laughing about it."

We both have a laugh over Dex's early years. "But no. I don't think you're crazy at all."

"I wish I could explain what the night was like. That night in Key West. It meant more to me than just, you know, sex."

"If things wouldn't have happened the way they did, you wouldn't be sitting here with me right now. In fact, what's his address? I think I need to send him a thank you note."

"For what?"

"For giving me the opportunity to show the woman who once loved him what an epic mistake he made. For giving me the opportunity to show the woman he once loved what a night of passionate sex is supposed to feel like. How much her beautiful body deserves to be pleasured. What it feels like to orgasm so much and so hard that she forgets her damn name."

"It's like he freed me that night. From my self-doubt, my guilt, my loneliness. He showed me what it's supposed to feel like when you're with someone who truly wants to be there." I shake my head, my eyes beginning to water. "I knew that night that Michael never truly wanted to be with me. Nothing we did was anything like that night with Dex."

Rory's eyes fixate on mine. "You mean to tell me my brother is more than just a hornball?"

That makes me laugh. "Yeah." I nod. "He's much more than that. Rory, he delivered our kid all by himself. He helped me through it and he didn't run. Fuck, if he hadn't shown up when he did..."

Rory shakes her head, bewildered. "I've seen my brother do some amazing things over the years, but hell if I can picture him delivering a baby. His baby no less."

"Well, I would be lying if I said it was all glitter and rainbows. I'm sure I said things that night that I'll never remember, but I do recall him mumbling something about grip gloves and hoping she wasn't too slippery." I laugh. "God, at least I can laugh about it now."

"He really wanted to be here that first night you were home."

My shoulders fall. "What? Why didn't he say anything? He could've stayed."

She shrugs. "I think he didn't know what to do because you guys hadn't talked about it. He didn't want to encroach on your space with your mom here."

"Fuck." The tears welling in my eyes finally spill over. "I had a feeling he wanted to stay and I didn't ask him to. I wanted him to stay, Ror. Having him with me in the hospital for those couple days was...it was everything. I didn't have to lift a finger. He was so damn sweet and all I wanted to do was ask him to crawl in bed with me, but you know, he's Dex and hospital beds are only so big."

"Oh, God. The visual. I can't!" She laughs.

"But I started to have real feelings for him. Strong feelings. And then when he was here the other morning, I heard him talking to Summer through the baby monitor about me."

"I think I really like your mom, Summer Grace."

"And I fell for him even more."

"And you haven't told him any of this?"

I shake my head. "I didn't want to put myself out there only to be told he doesn't have time for me. For us. I mean I would understand, of course, but it would hurt nonetheless."

"Oh Tate." Rory leans forward and grabs my hand. Summer stirs slightly in her arms but remains asleep. "I promise you; he'll never tell you he doesn't have time for you. Is his schedule busy during the season? Yes. But you have me. And Nina and Shelly at work, and you have Charlee, and Carissa when she can be here. You'll never be alone." She squeezes my hand. "Tate, I think Dex really wants this. I've seriously never seen him like this...like the way he is now, with Summer. With you. I think you should really talk to him."

I swallow my nerves and dry my eyes. "If you think I should, I'll do it."

"Eeeeeek!" she squeals softly. "Yes! I think you totally should. And then I can be all Dex and Tatum sittin' in a tree," she sings.

F-u-c-k-i-n-g...

God, waiting six to eight weeks post-partum might just kill me.

ME

pic of Summer wearing onesie that says, My favorite hockey player is Daddy.

DEX

Damn straight, Tater Tot! How are my girls?

ME

Ready to watch you and the guys crush it tonight! Go Red Tails!

DEX

We're feeling good! Should be a fun night.

ME

Score one for me and Summer.

DEX

I'll do my very best! You guys need anything?

ME

You mean besides the new TV, the bath items, the books and the snacks? 😌

DEX

I don't like not being there.

ME

I know you don't. But you have a job to do. Don't worry about us.

DEX

I'll never not worry about you, Tate.

ME

Does it make you feel better to tell you Charlee and Rory are keeping me company and taking great care of us?

DEX

Mildly better, yes.

ME

Go bring home another win.

ME

Update: Summer completely blew out of that cute onesie. Baby poop: 1 – Onesie: 0

DEX

Make that two blowouts then. Fuck, that was a rough game.

ME

You'll get 'em next time. Is Hawken okay?

DEX

Yeah. Banged his shoulder against the glass pretty hard but doc says there's no major damage. He's out for tomorrow's game.

ME

That sucks. I hope he makes a quick recovery.

DEX

So, tell me something about Summer. Did she hit any milestones today?

ME

Yeah, at two weeks old, she said (in her best British accent) "Mummy, can we have some tea and biscuits while we watch Daddy's game?" And then she rolled over several times and sat up all on her own.

DEX

LOL! I always knew she was gifted. God, I miss you guys.

ME

It's only game two. You have four more to go. Don't miss us so much that you can't focus.

DEX

No promises. I never imagined this would be so hard.

ME

That's what she said.

DEX

Ooooh! LMAO! You got me! 😆

ME

DEX

You should get some sleep.

ME

She'll be waking up within the next hour to be fed. No rest for these breasts.

DEX

wags eyebrows hubba hubba ding ding!

ME

🙄 Trust me, you don't want these milk bags.

DEX

Tatum, I would take you any way I could get you.

ME

You can say that now. You're hundreds of miles away.

DEX

Then I'll be sure to say it when I'm standing right next to you.

ME

Video of Summer awake in her crib

DEX

There's my tater tot! Fuck, I miss her so much.

ME

Thought you would like to see her awake for once.

DEX

Thank you for this. I'll watch it over and over until I fall asleep. Oh, and Hawken says hello.

ME

Hi to Hawken! How's he feeling?

DEX

Much better. Three more games and we're all feeling great. Hey, did you get my package today?

ME

I did, yes. It's lying right next to her everywhere she goes.

DEX

Good. I didn't want her to forget me.

ME

I'm not sure how that could possibly happen. You're pretty unforgettable.

DEX

You think so?

ME

Mhmm.

DEX

I could say the same to you.

ME

What makes me unforgettable?

ME

Hello?

ME

...You still there?

ME

You must be lying. You seem to have forgotten about me already. 😊

DEX

haha sorry. I was lost in thought. Honest answer?

ME

Uh, Yes. Absolutely.

DEX

You did that finger thing, Tate. In Key West. You made me come so hard I saw stars. No one has ever made me come like that in my life and I haven't stopped thinking about it since.

ME

I'll have to remember that. For next time.

DEX

Are you saying there's going to BE a next time? 😳 😈

ME

G'night Dex.

DEX

Really gonna leave me hanging with that one, huh?

DEX

Sending me into tomorrow's game with blue balls.

DEX

sigh Night Tatum 😔

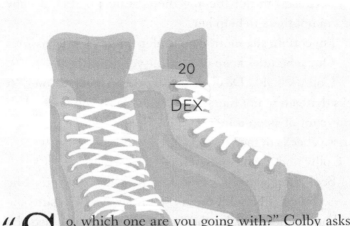

"So, which one are you going with?" Colby asks as he works through his game day bowl of Lucky Charms. "The bumblebees or the unicorns?"

I scroll through my phone studying every baby theme this warehouse has to offer. I've looked at everything from safari animals to teddy bears, to lady bugs, to mermaids. Although it would all do the trick, and most of it is cute, each in its own way, it doesn't scream Summer Grace Foster.

"I really have no idea," I answer with a shake of my head. "I want it to be perfect, you know? I want it to be just for her, but I want to put my own touch on it. I don't want it to look like I just bought everything off the showroom floor. I want it to mean more than that."

"Alright, so if you could make it anything you wanted, what would you do?" Milo asks.

"Fuck, if I know." I lay my phone down and rub my hand over my face. "I'm not a designer. I'm a hockey player. That's all I know. God, I feel like I'm failing her right now."

"How so?"

"Because I'm not fucking there! Tate just had a baby and I'm not there to help her."

"I'm certain she more than understands," Colby assures me. "Our schedules keep us very busy."

"Colby's right, Dex." Milo sits down next to me. "It sucks that you're not there, yeah, but at least you know she's got a team of people helping her. Rory. Charlee. I'm sure Carissa checks in too."

Colby nods. "She does. Three times a day."

"See? Stop worrying. She knows where you are. She knows you can't be with them right now. And I'm sure she also knows they will be the first two people you see the moment we're back in town."

Ain't that the truth.

Zeke pats my shoulder as he walks by. "As for this redecorating project, why wouldn't you put a little bit of you in the room?"

"What do you mean?"

"I mean literally, man. Hockey isn't just for boys. You know that. It can still be cute and girly but have your personal touch in there. You get to do whatever the hell you want. And whatever you do, I guarantee you, Tatum will love it."

"You think so?"

"I know so."

I pick up my phone again and send a text to my sister.

ME

I need your help.

RORY

How's Hawken feeling?

ME

He's good. A little sore but he's working it out.

RORY

Good. That was a hard hit the other night.

ME

Yeah. He's a lucky SOB.

RORY

So, what do you need help with?

ME

Gift for Tatum.

RORY

LOL another one? What is it this time? A basket of vibrators?

ME

Does she need a basket of vibrators? I can make that happen.

RORY

I don't think that's something brothers and sisters talk about.

ME

But it's something girls talk about. Don't tell me you don't because I know you do.

RORY

Fair

ME

Soooo?

RORY

Pretty sure she has at least one. Other than that, I think she's waiting for another tool.

ME

There's another tool? You have to tell me what it is. I'll send it to her. Whatever she needs.

RORY

Dumbass. 😂 Pretty sure that tool is YOU.

ME

Oh.

RORY

Yeah. Oh!

ME

Did she say that?

RORY

In not so many words...maybe.

ME

She likes me????? Like, she likes me, likes me???

RORY

You know I'm supposed to be teaching kids, right?

ME

But you didn't answer me and just tell those kids you're talking to your hot shot celebrity brother.

RORY

I just threw up in my mouth. Also, they're Kindergarteners, Dex. They don't give a shit who you are. They just want to eat paste and sing the birthday song.

ME

sigh fine. Fine. But listen. This delivery will be the biggest one yet. Gonna have some furniture delivered to the penthouse tomorrow.

RORY

Okay...

ME

Nursery furniture.

RORY

*GIF of little kid in Penguins jersey shouting YAAAASS"

ME

You know I hate that GIF, right?

RORY

You know it's my favorite right? 😊

ME

Ugh you kill me. Anyway, Think you can help with a little designing? I'll send you a few ideas I'm thinking about, but I want to incorporate hockey into the space as well.

RORY

Leave it to me! Charlee and I (and Carissa when she's back) will make this happen. Eeeek! I'm so excited!

ME

Thanks Rory.

RORY

Good luck tonight!

ME

One more night! I get to see my girls tomorrow!

TATUM

GIF of smiling heart

ME

I know it could be late, but I would really like to see Summer. And you. Would it be alright if I came over when I'm back in town?

TATUM

Of course! You don't even have to ask.

ME

I don't want you to wait up, in case I'm late. I have the key you gave me. I'll just crash on the couch.

TATUM

You don't have to do that Dex.

ME

It's fine. I don't mind. I just want to be close to my girls.

TATUM

Then join me. In my room.

Not wanting to have this discussion via text message, I tap Tatum's number and call her.

"Hey." Her soft sultry voice on the other end of the line sends my body into a beating pulse. Like if I close my eyes, I can feel her through the phone. Fuck, I've missed her.

"Do you really mean that?"

"Mean what?"

"Sharing your room? Your bed? You want me to stay with you?"

"If it's not what you want, it's o—"

"Tate?"

"Yes?"

"I'm going to need you to answer my question. Do you want me to stay with you?"

"I...I think Summer would love having you nearby."

I squeeze my eyes closed. "But would you, Tate? Would you love having me nearby?"

Just fucking say the words, Tate, and I'm there.

"Yes. I would."

I release a huge sigh of relief.

Just the words I needed to hear.

"Then I'll be there. I'll stay. Whatever you want, Tate. Whatever you need."

There's a silence on the other end of the line and then her soft voice says, "Dex?"

"Yeah?"

"Can I ask you something? A personal question?"

"I'm an open book for you, Tatum. Ask me anything."

She clears her throat and takes a minute before she finally asks, "Have you...I mean it's fine if you have. We've never talked about it one way or the other, but you know, while you've been away, have you...spent time with... anyone else?"

The nervousness and apprehension in her voice do not go unnoticed. She's seriously worried that I might be fucking my way around the country.

"Are you asking me if I've slept with anyone?"

"I mean, you have every right, Dex. I shouldn't even be asking it's just that—"

"Tatum Grace."

Light sniffles come from the other end of the line and my heart breaks into a million little pieces. "Yes?"

"I haven't so much as looked at another woman since before you stepped back into my life. And you can ask any one of the guys about that. Or Rory. They'll all tell you. I was a mess after Key West. I was infatuated with you. And when I finally saw you again and after, you know, everything, I promised you whatever you needed, whatever you wanted, I would be here and I mean that."

"What if what I need...what I want... is you?"

"Fuck, Tatum." I inhale a deep breath and let out a shaky one, trying not to smile too hard. "You have me. Fuck, do you have me."

"I don't want to do this parenting thing alone. If there's a chance that something might be there...between us then—"

"Hell, yes, there's a chance. There's more than a chance, Tate. I swear to God, I'll give it my all for you. I'm sorry I'm not there. I am. It's killing me to be away right now. I feel like I'm failing you at every turn."

"What? No. Dex, it's okay. You're not failing me at all."

"A good father would be there twenty-four-seven, Tate."

She huffs a soft laugh. "A good father loves his kid,

Dex. With his whole heart. It doesn't matter how many minutes are spent in physical proximity. You have a job to do that provides for her. Where would she be if you didn't?"

"She would have you."

"Well lucky for her, and for me, it's not just me. We have you. So, stop worrying, okay? Just because you travel for work doesn't mean you're a bad father. You've been one hundred percent zoned in on her since the moment she came out of me. You're a wonderful father. And you'll continue to be a wonderful father. Are you hearing me?"

How does she do it?

How does she calm the storm inside me before it even hits?

How has she turned my life completely upside down, yet I yearn for more every damn day?

"Dex?"

"I hear you." My words come out a choked whisper. "I hear you."

"Okay."

I hear Summer crying in the background. "Is she okay?"

"Yeah. It's just time for her to eat again. I'm sorry. I should go."

"Absolutely. Yeah. Do what you have to do."

"I'll see you tomorrow night?"

"I promise you will. I'll try not to scare you."

"G'night Dex. We'll be watching you play."

"G'night Tatum."

21

TATUM

It's twelve-thirty when I feel his strong arms lift me from the couch. The smell of his cologne wafting into my nose as I snuggle into his chest.

His bare chest.

My eyes open lazily and I peer up at him as he carries me to my room.

"You're home."

He kisses my cheek. "I'm here, Tate. I'm home."

"How long have you been here?"

I can barely see his smile in the darkness of my room. "Long enough to kiss Summer and get ready for bed before I came to get you."

I reach up and wrap my arms around his neck inhaling him. "I'm really glad you're here."

"Me too, Babe." He lays me down and then slides into my bed next to me. I turn toward him, nuzzling into his side. "Fuck, it feels good to finally be able to hold you."

If it's possible for my entire body to swoon, it just did. He makes me feel cherished. He makes me feel safe. He makes me feel like anything I could ever want out of this life is possible when I'm with him. His finger under my chin, he raises my head against his shoulder until he can see my face and then his lips are on mine soft, but demanding, hungry. His tongue slides against my lips and I open them welcoming him in and deepening our kiss, but what I feel from him isn't what I expected.

He isn't the primal man he was last summer.

This isn't the carnal side of Dex Foster I once experienced.

This kiss is different.

He's different.

He's telling me how much he missed me.

"Tatum." My name is a whisper as his hands slide gently down my body. I whimper at his touch because damn if I don't want this man. All of him. I want to remember what it was like with him many months ago. I want to remember how it felt to be free with him. I want to relive the feeling of being alive and uninhibited with him. "Fuck, I've missed you."

He grips the back of my neck and tilts my head, his tongue delving deeper inside me, swallowing my moans and feeding me his.

"Dex."

He pulls me over him so I'm straddling his hardened cock and fuuuuuck if it isn't hard. I nearly forgot what it felt like.

"Are you still bleeding?"

"A little." I nod, disappointed.

He must see my sadness because he brings his palm to my cheek and says, "Hey. It's okay. We don't have to do anything tonight. I'm perfectly content right here. I just want to be near you. Touch you. See you. I never thought I would hate being away from someone but this week fucking gutted me."

"Dex." I lean down to press my lips against his again and when I do, my body shifts over his cock and, "Oooh. My. God." I gasp. "You feel so incredible."

Slowly, I move my hips against him, the friction sending my body into a frenzy of need and desire.

"Yeah? You like that?"

"Mhmmmmm."

I sit up now, his hands on my hips as he guides me over his cock and back, again, and again, and again. "Dex, this body hasn't seen much action in the last nine months and I am a desperate, desperate woman."

"You need to get off, Tate?"

"Like. You. Wouldn't. Believe."

"Then ride me, baby. Take me. Use me. Whatever you need."

He lifts his hips and I rock against his cock, the pressure on my clit just enough to give me the friction I need. Dex lifts my t-shirt over my head and reaches for my nursing bra but I shake my head.

"Dex, they'll leak."

"Good. Let them. I'm not afraid of a little breast milk. I play hockey, remember? Trust me, I've seen some awful shit and this ain't it. Free yourself, Tatum. Allow yourself to feel what you want to feel. I'm right here. I'll give it to you. Anything you want."

I dry hump him while he helps me remove my bra and though they're a little sore, I have to admit, freeing my

232

heavy breasts from their constant bondage does feel amazing. Gently he brings his hands to the sides of my breasts, fondling them softly. My head falls back and my mouth opens as I moan through my pleasure and that's when it happens. Milk draining from my nipples. Down my body. On Dex's body. On his face.

God!

"Fuck! I'm sorry, Dex. I'm so sorry." I move to climb off him and clean myself up but he holds me against his cock, thrusting up against me.

"Don't you dare apologize."

"Dex."

"Tatum, look at me."

I don't want to meet his eye but I do what he asks because I know he won't back down.

"This body right here," he says, moving his hands up and down my rib cage. "This gorgeous body carried our child. Our *child*, Tatum. You did that. You carried her in this body and when the time came this body gave birth to her, and if that isn't a magical, beautiful thing, I don't know what is. And after all that, your body still feeds and nourishes her. Tatum, I watched your body do things I never imagined I would see in my lifetime and although at the time, I was a little freaked out and scared, as you were, I was and continue to be in awe of you. I'm not running away. I'm still here, and I want you. Okay?"

I don't answer him.

But I hear him.

"What's happening here is fucking natural and I'm not bothered by it one bit. All I care about right now is you, Tatum. Your pleasure. Your happiness."

"But—"

"If you sucked me off and I came in your mouth or all over your chin, would you swallow it down?"

"You know I would."

"Then how is this any different?"

"I..."

"There's no judgement here, Tatum. Let yourself go. I'm not your ex."

Tears spill down my cheeks. "I know you're not. You're a million times better than he ever was, Dex."

"That's right baby." He shifts me over his cock with a hungry grin. "So, make a mess. I'll clean it up. I don't fucking care. This, whatever this is between us, this is what I've craved for months so take me. Use me. Grind on me. Spray my face, I don't care. Just let go and take what you want."

And so I do, and this time I don't stop. I don't stop until I'm coming against him, suppressing my moans so as not to wake the baby, and finally finding the relief I've so desperately needed.

Afterwards, he starts a warm shower for me and helps me step in, and then changes the bed sheets while I'm enjoying the warm water. He joins me for a quick wash and rinse. Never once pursuing more. He washes my hair and soaps my body, never asking for a thing in return. All I can think about when I'm lying in his arms before drifting off to sleep is how much I don't deserve Dex Foster, but I'll be damned if I don't return the favor for all the love and compassion he's shown me since he reentered my life. He deserves to let go too. He deserves to feel free the way he encourages me. I need to see him, hear him, and feel him fall apart at my touch again. And I need it to happen soon.

Maternity leave came and went faster than I ever could have imagined and I do not like the idea of leaving my baby for an entire day so that I can go sculpt the minds of other peoples' kids. Ugh, when did I become so heartless? Or is it just that my heart is so full of Summer that I'm having trouble making room for anyone else?

Yeah.

That's got to be it.

When I set out for Chicago late last summer, I thought this year was going to be a year of soul searching. A time of unbridled adventure. Meeting as many people as possible and making the most of my life, and then Summer happened. Now I can't picture my life without her in it. Now, all I see when I look at her is pure joy and more love than I ever thought myself capable of giving to someone. I've heard it said that adults don't know love until they have a baby, and while that might not be true for everyone, it's certainly true for me. I would do absolutely anything for my little girl. I would walk through fire for her as would her daddy.

Dex has been here almost every waking moment he's not on the ice. The minute he walks through the door he takes Summer in his arms and gives me a break, whether it's a shower or a snack or some quiet time to read a book. He's been a godsend and I am more appreciative of him than he could ever know. He was also instrumental in my not freaking out about having to leave Summer to go back to work. He registered Summer for the daycare housed in the arena and so far, he's taken her with him to work every morning. At least if I can't be close to her every day, one of us can.

"I swear to God the booger brigade is out to get me today." Shelly makes her way to the sink and washes her hands, lathering herself in soap all the way to her elbows. "They've done nothing but sniffle and cough all morning. God forbid they cover their mouths."

"T'is the season," Rory says, tossing a grape into her mouth.

Nina stops scrolling on her phone and points out last night's hockey score. "How many more games until Dex comes home this time?"

"Seven," Rory and I both answer at the same time, giggling at each other across the table.

"Sorry." Rory shrugs. "Force of habit."

"Seven." Nina cringes after swallowing a bite of her sandwich. "Ugh, that must be hard on you, Tate. You guys doing alright?"

"Yeah, we're okay. Their first away stretch was rough but at least now I know what to expect. It's a bit of a pain in the ass to have to drive into the city to drop Summer off at daycare and then drive back out to get here, but we're making it work. Charlee and Rory have been great too, so I'm not always alone."

Focused on drying her clean hands, Shelly answers, "Meh. It gets easier the more kids you have. Maybe you just need to have another one."

236

I laugh. "You bite your tongue, woman. I just got my body back and I'm feeling like my old self again. I want to live in that for at least a little while."

"Suit yourself."

Rory smirks. "Now we just have to get Tatum to her very first Red Tails hockey game."

"Ooooh," Nina sings. "I bet Dex would love that."

"He's definitely been itching to get me there, but he's been very understanding of Summer's needs. And mine while I was on maternity leave."

"He's a good guy," Nina swoons.

"He is." I narrow my eyes at Rory. "Does he really dance to Taylor Swift before every game?"

"Every. Single. Game. It's like his pregame ritual or something."

"You mean like Colby Nelson and his Lucky Charms? Dex told me about that."

"Yeah, kind of like that. They all have their own thing. It's weird but if it helps them win, then, more power to them." She nods.

"If you need a babysitter, I'm more than willing."

"Thanks Nina. But I guess Dex has already worked it out for Summer to stay with the daycare in the building whenever I come to a game. Several other kids stay there too. Kids of other players and staff. So at least I know she'll be in the building close by. Dex wanted to make sure I would have the night off so I can relax and have fun at the game."

"Well, that's incredibly sweet of him." She smiles.

I send a quick wink to Rory. "He's been way more attentive than I ever expected him to be. He cooks dinner when he's in town and he spends his free time with Summer even if I'm working. He's really a great dad."

"Aaaaand?" Rory prods.

"Aaaaand, during his last away game stretch, he told me he wanted more. That he wanted...me."

Nina squeals next to me, clapping her hands excitedly while Shelly nudges Rory's elbow and smiles.

"Soooo we're officially together."

"YAAAAS!" Nina pumps her fist and Rory swipes her hand across her forehead.

"Phew, that took a while to say, huh?"

"I'm sorry." I cringe with a laugh. "When I left Michigan to move to Chicago, I was excited for a new job, a new home, and a new me. Getting knocked up by a professional hockey player and having his child wasn't exactly part of my plan."

Rory reaches for my hand across the table. "But you've handled it with grace and all the bad-assary you have in you and I, for one, am very proud of you and happy for you aaaaand thankful because now I get to be the super cool aunt!"

"Well, I don't know about badass, but Grace is my middle name."

"So, are you excited about your first hockey game? I can't wait to see how happy Dex will be to have you there."

I can't help the maniacal laugh that escapes my mouth. "Oh, Rory. How you underestimate my ability to pull a fast one on your brother."

Her eyes grow huge. "What? What does that mean?"

"Oh, you'll see."

"Look at her lifting her little head up like that!" Carissa squeals as she and Colby and Hawken step into the daycare room behind me

"I know, right? She's my little overachieving champ. Tatum says she should only be hitting that milestone around now, at eight weeks, but she's been doing it for a couple weeks." I lay my hand over my heart and pretend to cry with pride. "She's truly gifted."

"Must take after her mom," Colby teases.

"Fuck you, dude," I mumble. "She gets her beauty from her mommy. I'll give her that, but her brute strength? Yeah, that's all me."

I crouch down and smile wide as I scoop my princess into my arms. She smiles at me as her hand holds tight to my t-shirt. "Hey, Tater Tot! How's daddy's favorite little girl, huh? You look so cute in your little hockey pjs. Yes, you do," I coo at her as we walk to the door where I sign her out and let Kara, the nursery worker, know I'll bring her back down before her next feeding time.

"It's almost time for Daddy's pregame dance party."

Hawken raises a brow. "You're including Tater Tot in your Tay-Tay party?"

"Absolutely!" I smile at my beautiful girl. "She's the world's newest Swifty, and she's my good luck charm, aaaaand her mommy is coming tonight and I'm feeling good. So yeah, we're dancing it out." I pull the locker room door open. "So, get your ass in there, Malone."

"Cover your dicks, gentlemen! There's a girl in the room!"

"Smallson's been in here a gazillion times, Dex," Quinton laughs.

"Smallson's eyes may be permanently damaged, but she's an adult who can handle her own shit. My baby's eyes don't need to be scarred by your teeny weenies so cover 'em up."

I walk through the room with Summer Grace in my arms, and the guys all turn to mush around me, cooing and waving and offering her high fives as if she's old enough to clap back. I'm not really complaining though. The guys love my kid and they've been more than supportive of Tatum and me these last few months. I can't ask for more than that.

Except for when it comes to dancing it out to Taylor Swift.

I hand Summer off to Carissa while I dress for the game but before I pull on my jersey, I crank up the volume on my Bluetooth speaker and help to energize the team with a dance party. After dancing with Carissa, Zeke, and Hawken, Summer is back in my arms. I hold her gently against me and dance with her while I sing into her ear.

I feel like I could win this entire game myself.

I'm on cloud nine today and nothing could possibly bring me down.

The roar of the crowd outside the tunnel is intense. Whatever pregame activities are going on out there tonight, the energy in the arena is high and we can all feel it. Tonight's game against Detroit should be a great game, but it won't be handed to us. Their team is fierce and they've got some damn good players.

But ours are fucking better.

We currently have nobody off the roster. Everyone is healthy and accounted for and after coming home from a seven-game win streak, we're thrilled to be back home.

"You excited to see your girl?" Hawken smirks next to me. I can't stand still. I'm itching to get on the ice. To feel the sting of the chill on my cheeks, mixed with the heat of the crowd. Thanks to Summer getting a little cold a couple weeks ago, Tatum stayed home during our few home games, but tonight she is finally free to see me play and I couldn't be more thrilled.

"Fucking right I am. If I'm ever scoring a hat-trick, tonight is the night."

"You think?"

"I do. I've got this. I'm not holding back. It's time to kick some ass and take some names."

"Huddle up!" Nelson shouts.

The team circles around him and listens intently as he

gives us our pregame pep talk while the announcer begins his spiel in the arena. Right before we're called out of the tunnel, our hands meet in the center of our circle and we shout, "HUSTLE, HIT, and NEVER QUIT!"

"Let's hear it for our CHICAAAAAAGO RED TAAAAAAAAILLLLLS"

The team flies out to raucous applause from the crowd and circles the ice and then back around our net where Zeke awaits our warmup passes. I'm immediately in the zone going through our drills, watching the puck as we pass and shoot toward the net for Zeke to block.

"Yo, Dexter!" Quinton calls out to me. "What's with your girl?"

"Huh?"

He points to where Tatum, Charlee, and Rory are all sitting behind the glass right behind Zeke. Charlee wearing Landric's jersey and Rory's wearing one of Malone's he gifted her for Christmas when she whined about wearing mine. But Tatum...

"Son of a bitch. You've got to be kidding me."

Right there next to them, Tatum cheers on the Red Tails in a Detroit jersey.

Fucking Hell.

I skate toward them and smack my palm on the glass. "What the hell is going on?"

"Hey hottie! You look damn good in that uniform!"

No, no, no. She's not getting away with this that easily.

Compliments will get her nowhere tonight.

"What the fuck are you wearing?"

She shrugs innocently. "What? I'm from Michigan."

"Not tonight you're not. Take it off. Now."

She scoffs out a laugh and shakes her head, shouting back at me. "I'm not going to just take my shirt off, Dex. That's ridiculous."

"I didn't bring my girl into this arena to watch me play just for her to root for the other team! Take it the fuck off."

She doesn't say a thing in response. Just smirks at me and then blows me a kiss.

"Mother fucker!"

I push away from the glass annoyed that I'm even dealing with this right now when I'm supposed to be focused for the game, but I turn myself around and luckily spot the one person I know will help me. The one person who can get the entire arena's attention. If she wants to play games, I'm more than happy to oblige.

"Hey REMI!"

I sprint to the bench where our team mascot, Remi, the red-tailed hawk, is lurking for the beginning of the game. I toss off my gloves and helmet and pull my jersey over my head, not giving a rat's ass that I'm now shirtless on the ice. I find our equipment manager and shout for him to get me a new jersey. I grab a black sharpie from one of the staffers and write a quick note across my team number on the back and then shove the jersey into Remi's hands pointing down the ice to where Tatum is sitting.

"Section 109 at the glass. She's wearing a fucking Detroit jersey. Don't leave her until she's wearing my name, you hear me? Do whatever you have to do. And then make sure she gets one of every fucking piece of merchandise this arena has with my name on it. And take Smallson with you!"

Remi gives me a high five and turns to make his way up

and around the arena. Within minutes, Nick, our equipment manager, is back with a new jersey for me and I'm
redressed and back on the ice in time to finish the last
couple minutes or so of the team's warm-up. As both teams
are finishing, the music in the arena changes to Taylor
Swift's "Look What you Made Me Do", and Remi is now
on the jumbotron marching himself down the steps toward
the ice behind Zeke. Carissa follows behind, recording his
every move.

"Oh man. No, you didn't!" Hawken snickers when he
skates up next to me.

"Oh, I most certainly fucking did."

Remi finally reaches the bottom where Tatum is sitting
and offers her his hand. Smiling, she takes it and he leads
her out of her seat to the stairs where they have more room.
He tugs on her Detroit jersey and pretends to be sick all
over it as the crowd around them laughs. He shakes his
head *No* and then holds up my jersey turning it around so
she can see the back where I wrote on the large white
number seventy-seven.

My girl wears my name and my number.

He tugs on the jersey she's wearing once again and then
hitches his thumb behind him and the crowd around him
starts to chant, "Take it off! Take it off! Take it off!"

At least Tatum is a good sport about it. With a larger-
than-life eyeroll and a huge smile on her face, she lifts the
Detroit jersey over her head, leaving her long-sleeved
black t-shirt underneath. Then Remi helps her put mine
on. It's way too big on her but my dick twitches at the

244

sight of her finally wearing my number. Hawken nudges me.

"How's that feel?"

"Like I just fucking won." And that's no lie. I've seen thousands of women over the years wearing my name on their back, but it's never meant a damn thing to me before. They're just fans. Nobodies. I don't know any of them.

But seeing Tatum wearing my number...it's a whole new feeling for me. Because it means something to me. She means something to me. She is finally mine.

And I am hers.

The crowd cheers for Tatum who turns in a complete circle showing off her new gift. She lifts the collar to her nose and inhales and then smiles and hell, I could've come in my pants like a damn teenager watching her breathe in my scent.

"Dude, I think Dexter has a crush," Nelson says with a laugh as we all line up for the national anthem.

"I think it's more than a crush, Nelson," Landric answers. "Look at him. He can't take his eyes off her."

It's so much more than a crush. Much, much more.

"Well, he better focus on the damn puck once he hits the ice. You hear me, Foster?"

"Loud and clear, Nelson."

Landric faces off against Mindroni, Detroit's center. The puck is dropped and it's Landric's off the face off and he shoots it to Shay as Nelson and I scramble down the ice. Shay passes to Malone who takes his shot slipping the puck past Detroit's goalie for our first goal of the night.

"Holy shit!" Colby laughs as we join the group of them in a team hug. "That was like five whole seconds!"

"Always gotta be the showoff, huh Malone?" I beam at him.

"Hey, when you got it, you got it. What can I say?"

The game continues and we play through our shifts scoring once more before the end of the first period.

It's been a solid second period so far with the Red Tails maintaining the pressure against Detroit as Hawken and I come off the ice after our first shift. On the jumbotron, Remi appears in section 109 once again, a huge sack over his shoulder as if he's Santa Claus himself. He and Smallson descend the steps and the crowd cheers when he takes Tatum's hand and leads her to the steps for a second time. He digs his hand deep into his red sack and pulls out a Red Tails scarf wrapping it around her neck. Then he pulls out three different hats, a baseball cap, a beanie, and a toboggan, each of them sporting a Red Tails logo and makes her put on each one. She's such a good sport and though she looks silly wearing all her new team merchandise, I think she's fucking adorable.

Remi digs into his bag again and pulls out two other jerseys with my name across the back, a t-shirt, a long-sleeved t-shirt, and three hoodies all with my name on them. He tops her off then with a pair of sweatpants, two pairs of socks, two lanyards, one red, one black, a travel cup, a souvenir cup with bendy straw, a drink koozie, and last but not least, a large stuffed Remi the Red-Tailed Hawk wearing a team jersey.

The guys sitting next to me on the bench laugh at the spectacle Remi has made of Tatum while keeping their eye on the game play as it's almost time for our next shift.

"So, how are you feeling about tonight?" Hawken asks with a nudge to my arm.

"Fucking great."

"Yeah?"

I nod. "Yeah. The room looks amazing. I think she'll love it."

"Think she'll say yes?"

"Hard to say, but I fucking hope she will. It just makes sense, you know? It would be easier."

"Agreed. I really hope it works out for you."

"Thanks man. Hey, did Rory ask about chilling at your place tonight?"

"Yeah. It's cool. You know I've got plenty of room."

"Touch her and die though. I know my friends are her friends but she's still my sister."

Hawken shakes his head laughing. "Rory? That's cute, Dex."

"What's cute?"

"That you think you have any say in what she does these days. Have you met your sister?"

"Eh. You're not wrong, I guess. That girl is headstrong and too confident for her own good."

"Let's call it brave. She's brave."

I laugh. "That too. She's always forged her own path, God love her."

"I'm pretty sure it's never me you have to worry about," he says, and then we hit the ice for our last shift of the second period.

23

TATUM

Iknow I don't have much experience when it comes to attending professional hockey games but this has been one of the most fun days of my life. Getting to watch Dex and the rest of the Red Tails do what they do so close up is exhilarating, and they're playing tonight like they're on fire! I'm not sure how they can lose with a score of four to one, but I also know anything is possible.

I haven't been able to take my eyes off Dex all night. When he hit the ice before the game even started, I could feel his presence. I could feel his focus. And I have to give credit where it's due, because damn, does he look good in his uniform. Knowing I would be coming to the game tonight, I asked my brother to ship me a Detroit jersey because I knew Dex would react just as he did when he saw me in it. He might pretend to be the cuddly teddy bear when Summer is around, but the Dex I remember meeting in Key West wasn't gentle about anything and that's what I wanted to see again.

The possessive guy who wanted to make sure I knew I belonged to him.

I like a guy who doesn't share.

Dex Foster does things to me I can't even begin to explain.

With three minutes left to go in the third period, Charlee and Rory and I have been standing at the glass cheering our asses off for our team. For most of this period, the play has been near the other end of the ice as our guys have had control of the puck, but the pendulum swings and Detroit takes possession bringing the play back toward us.

Milo's in the middle of the ice and passes to Shay who shoots it to Dex.

"YES, DEX! LET'S GO!"

Dex turns wide to get outside the net, preventing Detroit from scoring. As he comes around to the other side of the net two of Detroit's players try to intercept his play and check him into the glass. At full speed there's no stopping them and the hit is hard. His shoulder hits the wall first and down he goes right in front of us and then it's a free-for-all fight for the puck. The flurry of action on the other side of the glass is intense. Each of them is shouting at their team-mates as sticks ram against each other in the fight for possession. Several players go down and there's a pileup on the ice.

"Where is Dex?" I shout.

Charlee and Rory look around for his number seventy-seven but none of us can see him.

"Did he end his shift?"

"No!" I shake my head. "He fell. He has to be down." I point to the pileup in front of us. "There!"

Another player trips and falls in front of us, his leg flying out behind him, his skate hitting Quinton's cheek as he leans in for the puck. We all gasp as spurts of blood spray from under Quinton's face shield and he screams in pain, grabbing his face and falling to the ground. The refs finally bring the game to a halt as some of the players are fighting, several have fallen on top of one another, and Quinton is being lifted off the ice by Hawken and Zeke, the team doctor already tending to the deep cut on his face.

"Dex? Where's DEX?"

As the fighting continues and players come off the bench to either join in or try to help, I finally spot Dex at the bottom of the pile up where players are scrambling to get their footing.

"DEX! Oh, my God! There he is! DEX!" Hunched over in a fetal position, Dex lays on the ice as one by one the other players are lifted away from him.

My chest tightens and my stomach threatens to lose the nachos and popcorn I had earlier as I look on helplessly.

"Is he hurt?"

Please God, don't let him be hurt.

Please, no.

Let him be okay.

Let him be okay.

Let him be okay.

"Why isn't he moving?"

What am I going to do if he's not okay?

Will it be serious?

Does he need a hospital?

I want to be with him.

How am I supposed to do this with...

God, Summer...

Your baby needs you, Dex.

Please get up.

You're going to be okay.

You have to be okay.

My hands are pressed against the glass and tears are now running down my face in fear.

"He's okay, Tate." Rory rubs my back. "It's okay. He's okay. I promise. He wasn't down long."

"Huh?"

I look out at the ice again and Dex is moving, rolled onto his back, Milo and Colby are at his side. He's talking to them as one of the doctors comes running out onto the ice. Before he gets there, Dex is already sitting up and talking to his teammates. I see him nod to them and to the doctor and then they're all helping him up as the crowd cheers for him.

And all the tension leaves my body in the form of sobbing tears...because that's what happens when you're a hormonal post-partum woman who has no control over her emotions. I stand there crying huge tears as my friends console me, promising me that Dex is okay and that everyone is alright, but at this point I can't stop them from coming. It's like my mind and my heart chose this moment to open the flood gates of the past year of my life. And now I'm a mess of emotions picturing myself raising Summer all alone because Dex is injured and no longer wants us in his life. My fears of him not thinking I'm enough for him hit me like a freight train and soon enough I'm having a mini panic attack right here in section 109.

"Tatum...Tate, look. Look up, Tate. Look at the glass.

251

He's okay." Charlee and Rory are coming at me from both sides. When I finally hear them enough to look at the glass, Dex is there on the other side, his gloved hand on the glass.

"I'm okay." He nods. "I'm okay."

Oh, thank God.

I nod back, wiping my stupid tears from my face with my shirt sleeve.

"Look at me, Tate!" he shouts. My glistening eyes connect with his and he gives me a sympathetic yet possibly worried grin. "I'm alright. Okay? I'll see you soon."

I nod back as do Charlee and Rory, and then he's swiftly escorted off the ice.

"Come on," Rory tells me. "There's only a minute left and he won't be playing anyway. We'll meet him by the locker rooms."

Charlee grabs my bag of Red Tails gifts and Rory takes my hand, leading me up the stairs and through the arena. Carissa meets us downstairs and escorts us to the hallway where the WAGS usually wait for their husbands after a game.

"What about Summer?"

"You and Dex can go and get her together. Give yourself a minute to give him a hug."

"Why didn't you guys warn me how scary this stupid sport is?"

All three ladies chuckle and Carissa speaks first. "I totally know how you feel. Colby took a cut to the wrist a year or so ago during playoffs. Got off the ice quickly with a trail of blood behind him, got stitches and got himself right back into the game. It was wild."

"These guys are crazy about their sport, that's for sure,"

Charlee says. "Milo will be lucky if his knees still work when he's fifty."

"Hey, ask Dex how many of his teeth are still his real adult teeth." Rory winks at me. "The man gets his teeth knocked out more than anyone I know. At least three in that ornery smile he has aren't even his God given teeth."

We wait in the hallway, making small talk for a solid twenty minutes or so before we see any of the players trickle out of the locker room. Colby and Zeke head to the press room for a few interviews. Quinton has been with the team doctor ever since coming off the ice and is now getting his cheek stitched up. Milo and Hawken file out of the locker room together and let us know Dex will be an extra couple of minutes. Coach wanted him checked over by the team doctors before he allows him to leave.

When he finally appears from the locker room, I don't even give him time to notice me standing here before I'm flinging myself at him, wrapping my arms around his neck.

"Tatum." He inhales and wraps his strong arms around my body, squeezing me to him tightly.

"You gave us a little scare there, Dex," Charlee tells him.

He smooths his hand up and down my back. "Yeah, I guess I did. Sorry about that." He lowers me to the ground, cupping my face in his hands. "But I really was okay."

"No major injuries, I take it?" Rory asks her brother.

He shakes his head. "A few bumps and bruises. They iced my shoulder while I was in there, but otherwise no. I'm good."

I shake my head. "We couldn't even see you for a while and then there you were in a fetal position."

He nods with a proud grin. "Fetal position is the best position to be in when a bunch of guys are piled on top of you. I knew I had to protect my head and I didn't want my skates cutting anyone if they fell so I brought them in as tightly as I could." He notices the tears welling in my eyes again and says, "I'm sorry I scared you."

He kisses my forehead and then gives me a sweet kiss on my lips. "But if it helps you feel any better, you look sexy as hell in my jersey...and scarf...and all three hats."

His comment makes everyone laugh and I'm finally able to dry my tears. "I'm sorry. It's the hormones."

He kisses my temple. "Don't apologize. You're fucking adorable. Now let's go get our baby and go home."

Yes, please.

"Where are we going?"

"Home."

"Uh, this isn't the way."

Dex smiles at me and reaches over to grab my thigh. "Just trust me."

We pull into the parking garage beneath his building. He carries Summer's car seat in one hand and holds mine with his other and together we make our way to the elevator and then to the top floor.

"I'd like to stay here tonight if that's okay with you." Dex says, unlocking the door.

"Uh...I...I mean I'm not against that, but where are we going to put Summer?"

"Hmm, that's a good question." He sets the car seat down on the couch once we're inside, unbuckling Summer and lifting her into his arms.

Gah! He's such a hot dad.

"Come here, I want to show you something." He takes my hand again and leads me down the hallway into the room across from the one I know to be his. He opens the door and flicks on the light and my breath catches at the sight before me.

"Oh, my God, Dex! Did you..." I step inside the stunning hockey themed baby nursery, trying to take it all in at the same time. "Did you really do all this?"

"I'm sorry it's taken so long. The girl's helped with a few design ideas but this is mostly my vision. Yeah."

Oh, my heart!

All the walls are painted white except for one. The stark white crib with red ruffled bedding rests against a black wall. Summer's name in large white letters is spelled out on the wall over the crib, each letter painted with tiny yellow suns that from a distance look like polka dots. Long red ruffled curtains hang from the two windows in the room and the crystal dimmed chandelier in the middle of the room casts a beautiful glow over the room. Perfect for our little sports diva. Along the other walls are framed hockey prints in black silhouette, one of them Dex's hand holding his stick. One of them, the back of him wearing his number seventy-seven.

"This is..." I shake my head, marveling at every beautiful detail. "This is amazing Dex."

He takes a moment to point out the dresser full of new baby clothes, and closet full of diapers, wipes, and bathtime accessories. It's truly a dream come true type of space and he's thought of everything. I spot the white rocker-glider in the corner of the room and the beautifully knitted red baby blanket laying across the armrest.

"This is beautiful. Where did you get it?"

He smiles. "I made it."

"You...what?" I unfold the blanket to get a better look. It's a bright red knitted blanket with a white trim line all the way around about a quarter of an inch in. "You made this?"

"Mhmm."

"That's right!" I recall. "I almost forgot you knit. Where the heck did you learn a skill like this anyway?"

He shrugs. "I couldn't keep my mind off you when I got back from Key West last summer. I had no way of finding you and it was...you know, it was hard. It got to me. I needed something to do with my hands that would also keep my mind busy, so I learned to knit. Little did I know the project I started knitting would turn into a baby blanket for my own kid."

My smile falters and my shoulders fall as he tells me his story. "Dex, I'm so so—"

"Don't be sorry. It's not your fault. We could've used real names, but we didn't. That was our choice and it's okay. Sit here with me while I feed Summer?"

"Of course."

After I went back to work, it became way too hard to find a time to be able to pump and as there were a few times Summer would sleep almost through the night, I made the decision to end sole breastfeeding. With the amount I pumped before returning, we've had enough to continue to use and now Dex can help with feedings, something he's really wanted to do.

He gets a bottle ready for her and then cuddles up with her on the love seat near the windows in her room. I take a seat next to them, my hand on Dex's knee as he gives her a bottle and opens up to me.

"I'm not like you, Tatum." He slowly shakes his head. "I don't come from a close family. I don't come from a big family. It was messed up and ugly at times. I basically raised Rory from the age of fifteen. Not because my mom wasn't around. She was. But she cared more about her next high or the drink in her hand than she did us."

"Oh, Dex."

"I'm not telling you this for pity, Tate. Clearly you can see I did pretty damn well for myself and I'll make sure Rory is set for life. I know teachers don't make nearly the money they deserve."

"How did you even get so involved with hockey then?"

"Call it sheer dumb luck, I guess?" He frowns. "My dad had all kinds of money and when he left, my mom got half so she was set. And she knew if she paid for Rory and me to do extracurricular things, it kept us out of her hair. So, she registered me for a young hockey league and Rory for dance lessons. Rory didn't give two shits about dance, but I actually found that I enjoyed hockey. And I was good at it. Coach kind of took me under his wing and the rest is history."

"Why are you telling me this, Dex?"

"Like I said, it's not for pity. I want you to know my past so you can know my future. Which, I really hope will be our future. I want you to see how much I'm trying to be here for Summer. For you. I want this, Tatum. I want this life with you."

His declaration makes me smile.

It also makes me want to jump his bones, but maybe not with a baby in his arms.

"I want those things too, Dex."

"I may not always be the best father. I don't know how to do any of this, Tate, but by God, I'm trying. I don't want to fail this precious little girl. And I don't want to fail you."

Rising to my knees, I reach over and cup his face in my hands. "You're not failing me, Dex. You've never failed me. Not once. We can do this together. We can make a great team. I believe in us."

His eyes glisten and I swear his chin trembles ever so slightly. "You don't know how happy I am to hear you say that."

Summer has fallen asleep taking her bottle. Dex lifts her onto his shoulder, patting her back until she burps and then together, we change her diaper and her clothes. Dex swaddles her and lowers her into her crib, kissing the side of her face before laying her down.

We stand together next to her crib watching her sleep and marveling at the precious baby we created. Staring at her never gets old.

Dex turns on the monitor and flicks off the light as we close her door halfway and then step into the hall. That's when he turns me against the wall and presses into me. His smokey eyes penetrate mine as his hand smooths down the side of my face.

"Please tell me I get to spend this entire night inside you."

I sigh against his lips, my eyes fluttering closed at his touch. "I was beginning to think you were never going to ask."

"Is that a yes?" He growls.

"Hell yes. Please, yes."

"Thank fuck," he moans as he lifts me, my legs around his waist, his hands on my ass, and kicks his bedroom door open carrying me into his room.

I set her down slowly, her body sliding against mine.
Fuck, she smells good.
Like ice.
Like Summer.
Like victory.
My hand cupping the side of her head, I kiss her forehead and then her cheek, her nose, and her chin and then I drop to my knees. Slipping a few fingers into the top of her leggings, I pull them down and help her step out of them, removing her heels only for a moment before helping her step back into them. When I stand up, she reaches for the hem of her jersey but I stop her.

"No. Leave it."

I step back and take a long minute to look at her. Really look at her. My jersey hangs on her body like a sexy dress, the hem covering the perfect curve of her ass. Her toned and bare legs lead to the red fuck me heels. Her long golden locks in loose waves over her shoulders hides the slope of her neck.

"Do you have any idea how stunningly beautiful you look right now?"

She doesn't respond so I continue. "Ever since I entered the NHL, I've had this dream. This fantasy of fucking someone wearing my jersey. And I don't mean my jersey like any old jersey with my name on it. I mean this moment, right here. The woman of my dreams, the one I would do anything for, wearing my literal jersey. With my name across her back. And my number and nothing else, while I'm balls deep inside her."

Pulling her bottom lip between her teeth, Tatum drags her arms inside her shirt, and reaches behind her back. Seconds later, she's tossing the black shirt she had on underneath my jersey as well her bra to the floor in a show that tells me she now has nothing on under that number seventy-seven.

"Well, Sir," she says, stepping up to me and laying her hand on my chest. "You are about to get very lucky because your wildest fantasy is about to come true."

"Holy fucking shit, Tate." I shake my head, marveling at her. "You make me so goddamn hard."

She stands on her tip toes and brushes her lips against mine and then whispers, "Then use me, Dex. You've given me so much and now it's your turn. Take me. Use me. Need me."

"I do need you, Tate."

I press my lips against hers in another kiss, slower this time, tasting her, deepening the connection we share with just the intimacy of our mouths until she's whimpering in my arms. And when I can't stand it any longer, I turn us both, hard, until she's pressed against the floor to ceiling window, the darkened lake and city lights below her only view.

Standing behind her I whistle lightly. "Now that is a view."

She might be looking at the lights and water below, but I have a full view of her gorgeous body covered in nothing but my name and it is fucking everything.

"Can anyone see me up here? Against this window, I mean?"

I moan my appreciation as I suck on her soft earlobe. "Do you want them to see you?"

She doesn't answer at first. I wrap her hair around my hand and pull her head back, exposing her neck while I sneak my hand around her waist and down between her warm legs. "Answer me."

"I..." She lets go of a heavy breath. "Dex, my body is on fire right now. If someone wants to watch, let them watch. I don't fucking care."

I'm impressed.

That's not at all what I expected her to say.

"Unfortunately, Tatum, I don't like to share, so no. You can see out, but nobody can see in. Rest assured you are mine, and only mine." I kiss the spot right behind her ear and then murmur, "Now, be a good girl and spread your legs for me."

Her breath catches but she does what I ask and I reward her with a finger against her wet swollen clit. "Christ, you're wet for me, Tate."

So goddamn wet.

"Yes," she breathes. "I've wanted this for a long time, Dex. Please don't make me beg."

Answering her plea, I reach back and pull my shirt off over my head and then sink down to my knees, positioning myself between her legs and peppering kisses up the backs of her thighs until I hit that sweet spot that makes her euphoric. Spreading her with my thumbs, I lean forward and take the first taste I've had of her way too long.

And she does not fucking disappoint.

"Just how I remembered. Fucking delicious, Tate."

"Oh, God!"

Her breathing picks up and she moans in pleasure, fogging the window. Unable to bear it any longer, I unzip my pants and free my strained cock, palming it in my hand and giving it a squeeze as I lick her again. And then I'm insatiable. Greedy. Ferocious. Ravenous. One drop of her and the room spins around me. I'm delirious and immersed at the same time as my number one goal becomes eating her out until she screams.

I start with long lethargic strokes against her with a flick of my tongue on her clit, again and again, and again until she's writhing over me.

"Dex! Oh, God...I can't..."

"You can baby."

I lap at her clit once, twice, three times and then suck. Hard.

"Fuuuuck, Dex." She leans her forehead against the window, the chill outside cooling her flushed face as she tries to control her breathing.

She's really bad at it by the way.

But I love her just like this.

Spinning out of control at my hand. With my tongue. And my name on her back.

SUSAN RENEE

I go in for the kill, swirling my tongue over her clit and then pushing inside her with two fingers, curling them against her inner wall.

And. I. Do. Not. Stop.

She moves her hips over my face, forward and back, forward and back working herself into a frenzy.

"Yes! Yes! Dex! I'm...I'm coming...Fuuuuck Dex!" She gasps and bites her hand as she comes over my mouth, my tongue enjoying every drop she gives me as her hips slow.

Christ, she has me so hard if I don't get inside her right now, I might blow like a fucking teenager. I waste no time standing up and then slip my hands under the front of her jersey until I'm holding both of her breasts in my hands.

"I need to be inside you, Tatum," I murmur against her. "I'm a fucking hungry man and I've missed you so goddamn much."

"Then what are you waiting for?" She pants.

"I don't want to hurt you, baby."

"I'm not going to break, Dex. Fuck me like you need to."

Jesus Christ.

This woman.

"Put your hands on the window, Tate. And brace yourself."

I pull her hips back a little and have to bend my knees slightly to line myself up behind her and with one feral thrust I'm sliding inside her. My eyes squeezing shut as I focus on how she feels.

"Tatum...shit. This isn't going to last long this first time, babe. I'm sorry."

She's nothing but moans and whimpers. "Sooo good."

Glancing down at our connection, I push as far inside her as I can until I bottom out.

"Fuck. So deep."

Her body takes my cock with ease. Like I was made for her and she for me and the thought that there is one person in this world made specifically for me and she's right here, naked in front of me, fuck...the idea sets my body on fire. If my cock can grow any harder it just did and I can't hold back any longer. She pushes back against me and it's the invitation I need to drive into her harder and harder, moving my hips forward to meet hers. At my next thrust, she clenches around me and I stumble against her, grasping her hips to steady myself.

"Fuck, Tatum. Do that again."

Her body tightens around me while I'm inside her, squeezing me, milking me, and I'm a goner. My balls start to tighten and ache, and I feel the surge at the base of my spine and before I know what happens, my orgasm is ripping through me and I'm a breathless, sweaty mess.

"You are gorgeous," I tell her as I kiss the small of her back, my cock still dripping inside her. "And you feel even more incredible than I remember."

Pulling out of her, I'm halfway to hard all over again, clearly not done reconnecting with the girl of my dreams. She turns in my arms and I lift my jersey over her head, marveling at her beauty. Her body is different now, and I can see the nervousness in her eyes when I gaze at her.

"What are you thinking?"

She swallows and crosses her arms over her chest.

"This isn't the same body you had fun with a year ago. Pregnancy took its toll. I'm sorry."

"I'm sorry?" My eyes grow large. "I'm sorry?" I shake my head. "Wait, wait, wait." I cup her whole face in my hands. "Surely you are not standing here in front of me apologizing for your body because of how you look now that you've carried and birthed our child."

"Dex, I—"

"I love you, Tatum."

Her big doe eyes stare back at me. She definitely wasn't expecting to hear that.

"Did you hear me?"

Wordlessly, she nods.

"Do I need to say it again?"

"I...yes."

"I love you, Tatum Lowe." I brush her hair back, my fingers playing with the ends. "I love everything about you. I love these new curves," I tell her, running my hands down her hips. "And these little marks right here." I trace a finger over one of her stretch marks. "These marks celebrate what your gorgeous body did for us. For me. For Summer. You're a warrior, Tatum. And besides, have you seen my body? It's covered in hockey scars from one accident or another. Did you know some of my teeth aren't even real?"

"Dex," she huffs a quiet laugh.

"Fuck, Tatum. I'm in love with you. All of you. I want you. I want you all the goddamn time. I want you with clothes on and with clothes off. I want you when I'm sleeping and when I'm awake. I want you on the ice and off. Every minute of every goddamn day. I want you. You're beautiful. Stunning. When you're around I have trouble keeping my eyes and hands off you. And don't get me started on what you do to this guy," I tell her, pointing to my now weighty erection.

Her eyes fall to my cock and her mouth falls open, her tongue gliding swiftly across her lips and I almost chuckle. She's like a lioness looking at her next meal and I'm fucking here for it. Her eyes meet mine and then they fall back to my cock. She walks me backwards until my legs hit my bed. She pushes me down and pulls off my pants and briefs and then gestures with her head.

"Against the headboard. Now," she demands.

Holy shit.

My girl's going all alpha on me.

And I don't hesitate for one fucking second.

I scoot myself back against the headboard, leaning back on the pillows, completely bare for her. My hardened cock resting on my stomach, a bead of cum drowning my Prince Albert piercing. Tatum climbs onto the bed and maneuvers over my body until she's sitting between my legs. She wraps her hand around my shaft and I close my eyes with a heavy sigh. "Fuck yes."

She strokes me from root to tip and then lightly licks the bead of cum from the head, her tongue swirling in a crazy eight pattern around the tiny silver barbell. Flexing my hip, I run my hand through her hair as she lowers her mouth over me.

"That's it, baby. Take me in. Suck me." My eyes roll back at the feel of her mouth around my cock. She takes me in with perfection, her tongue circling me as she squeezes the base of my shaft with her hand. "So fucking good." She pumps her mouth over me several times, taking me as deep as she can, her sucking noises making me even harder if that's possible. Just as she has me nearing the edge, she stops, gazing up at me under her hooded eyes. She bends each of my legs at my knees and spreads my thighs wide.

Mother fucker.

"Tatum..."

"I love you too, Dex. Let me show you."

She sinks down and rims my ass with her tongue and fuuuuck does that feel incredible. She sucks on each of my balls, and then runs her tongue up and over my cock, taking me all the way to the back of her throat. In my blissed-out state, I watch as she slides her hand between her legs, lubes her fingers in her own arousal mixed with my cum, and then circles my ass once again.

And then she gently presses a finger inside me.

I gasp a deep breath. "Fuuuuuck me, Tatum."

One hand holding the base of my cock, she sucks me into her mouth at the same time she presses her finger inside me...and then another.

"Fucking, Christ."

She doesn't relent. She keeps her pace. Tasting me. Touching me. Controlling me. Everything in me wants me to squeeze my eyes closed and lay my head back reveling in this magical feeling but damn it all to hell, I can't not watch what she's doing to me.

"Babe...fuck...I'm..."

My muscles tense with the acceleration of her speed. The slickness of her fingers, the pulse building inside me.

Slip, slide, squeeze, stroke.

Slip, slide, squeeze, stroke.

Slip, slide, squeeze, stroke.

"Oh, God."

"Fuck."

"Yessssss."

"Tatuuuuuum."

"I'm gonna...."

My mouth opens wide as I try to catch my breath. My cock swells, and I fear Tatum might choke and then I'm coming so damn hard I spring out of her mouth and spray her lips, her chin, her chest.

"Holy fucking...hell."

She pants and wipes my cum from her face, sucking on her fingers like they're candy coated, and pulls her other two fingers from inside me.

"I don't think I've ever come so damn hard in my entire life."

She gives me a drunk, satisfied smile and then leans forward on her knees to kiss my lips. "I love you, Dex Foster."

"I fucking love you, Tatum."

I wrap my arms around her and hold her tightly against me, my hands running through her hair and up and down her back as we take a moment to rest, and all I can think about is what a lucky son of a bitch I am. I owe Tatum's friend Eliza the world for encouraging me to hit on Tatum that night in Key West. I owe Tatum the world for making me a dad and for giving me the greatest, most precious gift she could ever give me. My life finally feels full. Like I have a purpose other than just lacing up my skates and hitting a puck with a stick.

I have a daughter. A sweet child who will always have me in her court. I'll bend over backwards to give her every happiness she could ever want. I'll be there to guide her through life and teach her to persevere. And I'll be the one to show her that no matter what kind of person she thinks she's meant to be, no matter who others think she is or should be, she gets to choose who she wants to be. She gets to choose her own path.

Just like I'm choosing mine.

"Move in with me." The words tumble so effortlessly from my mouth I wonder if I even said them out loud or if maybe I only said them in my mind.

Tatum slowly lifts from my chest, meeting my blissful gaze. "What did you say?"

"I said move in with me."

"Are you serious?"

"Fucking serious Tate. You're not that far from work. You could carpool with Rory. There's more than enough room here for you and Summer. I could take her to daycare with me every day."

"But...what about Rory. I can't just encroach on her space."

"Then we'll get our own space."

Her eyes grow even larger. "What?"

"Yeah. Let's buy a house. Be a family. Raise Summer together."

"I..."

"I love you, Tatum. I love you so goddamn much and I want to spend the rest of my life with you. I won't ask you to marry me if that's not what you're ready for but that doesn't mean we can't be together. I'm committed to you. To Summer. To this little family of ours. I want it all. And I want it with you."

"Are you sure this isn't some post-orgasmic high or something?"

I laugh. "No. I promise it's not." I lay a palm to the side of her face. "I want you, Tatum. I want you and Summer with me always. I know it's sudden and I know our relationship hasn't exactly been conventional, but it's not like we're two lovesick teenagers. We're adults. We're old enough to know what we want and make our own choices and I choose you, babe. I choose us. I want us. Please, say you'll move in with me."

She huffs a soft laugh and smiles back at me, shaking her head in disbelief. "You're really serious? You want this?"

"I want this more than I want the Stanley Cup in our arena."

"Whoa. Don't go jinxing yourself. Alright, alright. We'll move in."

With a huge smile on my face, I press my lips to hers and kiss her senseless. "Thank you, Tatum. Thank you for making us a family."

She moves across me, straddling my lap and wrapping her arms around my neck. "Thank you for giving me a man to hug and kiss."

I throw my head back in laughter. "Ben Dover loves Amanda Hugginkis."

Want more Tatum and Dex?
Visit my website for their extended epilogue!
www.authorsusanrenee.com

Want more of the Chicago Red Tails?
Turn the page for an excerpt of
Quinton Shay's story.

SAVING THE GAME EXCERPT

Quinton

"Dude, my love for you is like diarrhea," Hawken professes to Dex as he shoves a few more fries into his mouth to keep from laughing. "I just can't hold it in."

Clearing my throat, I pull Hawken's plate of fries away from him, grinning when he scowls at me as I slide the plate toward Dex. "Dexter I'm pretty sure your bromance boyfriend just said his love for you is shit."

Laughing, Dex grabs a few fries from Hawken's shared plate and tosses them in his mouth. "Trust me, I think I'm beginning to believe him. Chose my sister over me and everything."

"She's a lot prettier than you, and what can I say?" Hawken shrugs. "She sucks my dick better than you do, man."

Dex frowns and throws one of his fries on the table. "Fuck. And I watched tutorials for hours and everything."

Zeke nudges Hawken's arm, chuckling. "He means porn, bro. He watched porn for hours."

"Listen Dex, I've got this all figured out," I tell him with confidence. Lifting the hem of my shirt, I hold it out for him. "Feel my shirt. Do you feel that?"

Dex reaches out and rubs the fabric between his fingers. "Yeah."

"That's boyfriend material right there, man." I wink at him. "Fuck Hawken. There's a new bromance in town." Instead of the French fries Hawken's been gnawing on, I pass Dex my plate of pretzel bites and beer cheese.

The guys laugh as Dex rubs his chin pretending to consider my proposal.

"I do enjoy a good cheese," he says. "And if the next round is on you, I might just have to take you up on the offer, Quinton. Be a good boy and I might even let you grab my ass occasionally."

I sigh like a lovesick teenager. "Be still my heart. Of course, the next round is on me." I stand from our booth. "Be right back."

I head to the bar and order Dex and I another round, saying hello to a few of the mingling fans from out of town who aren't used to seeing the team hang out in a public bar. Pringle's has been good to us for years so most of the regulars know this tends to be our hangout spot. Occasionally though, we get a few newcomers who are shocked to see us here. We're just grateful we have a safe place to hang out and be ourselves once in a while and the management does a fantastic job of helping foster that kind of environment for us.

Cathy, the bartender, hands me my drinks and I thank

her, turning to walk back to our booth when someone catches my attention.

"Yes. Quinton, Mom. His name is Quinton Shay."

My head turns toward the female voice when I hear my name. A woman seated at the bar is talking on her cell phone. She's facing away from me so I can't see her face, but hearing my name always makes me take notice. My parents weren't going for normal when they picked my name. They couldn't just settle on Sean, Mike, or Jeff. Nope. They had to decide on a unique name that always had me standing near the back of the line in elementary school. Quinton is not a name you hear often these days.

"What do you mean what does he do? He's a famous hockey player. I told you that."

That's right babe. Just another famous hockey player.

"Oh yeah. He's a super great guy. Total dreamboat. The whole package," she says. My brows peak in response as I stand behind her eavesdropping.

Well, well, well. Dreamboat huh? Maybe I'm gettin' lucky tonight.

"I mean, his schedule is really busy, you know? With games and his charity work and all, so I don't get to see him every day but we've been together for about six months now."

My expression changes from amusement to shock and then right back to amusement.

Who the heck is this girl?

"Dinner?" she squeaks. "Umm, yeah. He might be able to do that."

I tilt my head, watching her from behind with morbid curiosity. She brings a palm to her forehead and sighs. "I'll

275

ask him but with short notice and all, you know...he might not be able to make it."

Wow.

This girl's got balls.

There's got to be a story here and I kind of want to know it.

For shits and giggles of course.

Noticing she's drinking the same thing I'm holding in my hand I linger a bit to listen to the end of her conversation, ignoring Dex's request for another beer.

"Alright. I'll see him in the morning but uh, I'll text him tonight and see if he can make it...yeah. Okay. Bye, Mom."

She lays her phone down on the bar, takes a deep breath, and then drains the rest of the drink in front of her. I know I could walk away from this. By all means I *should* walk away from this. Maybe it's just my lightened mood because of our upcoming All-star break or maybe I'm straight up stunned by this woman's audacity because last time I checked, I'm not only very single, but I also haven't been on an actual date in years. Whatever this is, I'm intrigued.

If the guys were to hear what just happened, they'd be egging me on to hit on the girl and have myself a fun night. Confidence is attractive in a woman and she surely has that, but something seems off the more I watch her. She's not joking with a friend. She's not texting someone else. Not talking to anyone else, so what gives?

Why the lie?

She finally turns and when I see her face I know I've seen her somewhere before. She's dressed in a pair of tight black pants. Maybe they're leggings, I can't tell, and an oversized sweatshirt that hangs off her shoulder. Her black bra strap is on display. Her chestnut brown hair is tied up in a messy bun, but it's the bandana bow that's making me scroll through my mental rolodex because I know I've seen this woman before.

I don't know what makes me to do it. Maybe sheer dumb curiosity but here I am sliding one of my beers in front of her.

No turning back now.

"So, we're meeting the parents, I hear?"

Her jaw hangs open when I lower myself into the seat next to her and she realizes who I am.

"Oh, my God!" She gives herself a face palm, a goofy smile on her face as she shakes her head. "I totally deserve this, don't I? This is what happens to people like me."

I take a sip of my beer and smile back at her. "People like you? Do you mean women who phone a friend or in your case, a parent, and lie to them about dating hockey players?"

"Shit. You heard all that?"

I laugh this time. "Kind of hard to miss when I was standing just a couple feet away."

"Oh fuuuudge." She brings her hands up to her blushing cheeks. "I am SOOO so sorry. God, you probably think I'm the biggest psycho." Her eyes grow into huge saucers. "I swear I'm not a stalker or anything."

"It's fine. Really," I tell her, mesmerized by her mossy green eyes. "Forgive me, but I feel like I know you from somewhere and I can't for the life of me figure out where. What's your name?"

She takes a sip of the beer I gave her. Part of me wants

to chastise her for accepting an open drink from a guy. I might be a famous hockey player but we're not all fine, upstanding men. "Oh. I'm Kinsley Kendrick. I took pictures at Hawken and Rory's wedding in the arena. Maybe you saw me there?"

"Yes!" I sit up taller, pointing my finger at her. "That's it. I remember now." She wore that pretty blue dress. "Sorry I didn't recognize you in casual clothing."

She slouches, slightly rolling her eyes. "Ugh, yeah, sorry. I don't usually dress up anymore unless I absolutely have to."

"Anymore?"

"My parents," she starts with an annoyed nod. "That's who I was talking to on the phone."

"Uh oh." I grin. "This doesn't sound good."

"If I tell you I grew up in L.A. where several celebrity families were our neighbors, does that give you any indication?"

"Ah, so you're a socialite." She narrows her eyes. "Ooor your parents are...or were?"

"In all honesty, I think my parents would scoff at the word socialite. They prefer words with a little more finesse."

I pass her a smirk. "So spoiled little rich girl doesn't describe you?"

She snorts and I smile because for whatever reason I think her little snort is cute. "Not hardly. I mean, if my parents had anything to say about it, I would be back in L.A. helping them run their empire and taking over when they retire, but their life is so far from what I want. That's why I moved here. Far away from them."

"Oh?"

"I've seen enough of that lifestyle to never want to be a part of it ever again."

"Why do you say that?"

She huffs out a light laugh. "Because the perfectly poised rich life just isn't for me. I'm more of a hot mess and happy kind of girl."

Interesting.

It's not every day you see someone who comes from money and does not want the life money can afford. Something about her demeanor draws me in though. Like she has layers I want to peel back one at a time as I get to know her.

"So, you were talking to your parents. Does that mean you're flying home to see them or something?"

"No." She shakes her head with a cringe. "They're in town for a few days on business and they want to meet my rich boyfriend. Because far be it for me to date a normal guy who has a normal job and makes an honest, normal wage." Realizing what she just said, she squeezes her eyes closed and cringes again. "Oh shit. I just put my foot in my mouth. I'm sorry, I didn't mean to say that you don't—"

"I totally get it," I reassure her. "Professional hockey isn't exactly on the list of normal jobs with a normal wage."

"Right, but it sure as hell made my mom happy to hear I'm not an embarrassment to the family and found a celebrity athlete to date instead of a local plumber, though I'm not positive she believes me. Not that I care at all. I'll tell her anything to keep her off my back so I can live my life in peace."

"So can I ask you something then?"

"Sure. I mean, I've pretty much laid my entire life story

out for you when you never really asked, haven't I?" She smiles. "Ask away."

"Why me?"

"What?"

"Why did you tell your parents you were dating me specifically."

"Uh..." She bites her lip to hide her nervous smile. "Because you're single aaand not at all hard to look at." She winces. "Aaaand you were the first person to come to my mind probably because I saw your post-game interview on T.V."

She's cute when she blushes.

"Well, that's as good a reason as any, and thanks for the compliment."

"No, I should be thanking you," she says as she smooths a hand down my arm. Her simple touch causes me to suddenly think about what it would feel like to have her hands all over me. Or really anyone's hands for that matter. Except for Dex. Not his hands. "For not getting someone to kick me out of this bar the minute you heard me tell my parents I'm dating you. According to my parents I'm a hot mess of one bad decision after another which is evident in the fact I just pulled a lie out of my ass to save myself from their wrath. I really am sorry and don't worry about a thing. I'll be telling them tomorrow that you caught a bug and can't make dinner."

I can't believe I'm doing this. "Or you could tell them I'm available."

She cocks her head. "I'm sorry?"

What the fuck am I doing?

"You said your mom probably doesn't believe you, so

why not shove her disbelief in her face? It just so happens, I'm free."

"Wait," she says, leaning back on her stool. "Are you seriously offering to be super petty with me to stick it to my parents to get them off my back?"

I laugh. "What if I told you my name was Quinton Petty Shay?"

Her eyes narrow. "Is it?"

"Not at all." I shake my head. "But this sounds like an opportunity too fun to pass up. If you're going to lie to them about us being in a relationship, go big or go home, right?"

"You're serious?"

"One hundred percent. I have the day off tomorrow. If you're in, I'm in. I could use a reason to have a little fun."

She considers it for a moment, an adorable smirk lighting up her face. I notice the cute dimple in her right cheek when she smiles. She really is quite pretty.

"Can we make up some crazy shit about how we met?"

"I wouldn't have it any other way," I tell her with a gentle laugh.

"Oh, my God, I can't believe I'm about to take you up on this kind of offer."

"Going once...going twice..."

"I'm in!" She laughs, taking another drink of her beer. "I'm so fucking in."

"Perfect. Let me give you my number and then you can text me the details."

"Okay. It'll probably be super upscale if that's okay. My parents would never step foot in a place like this."

Typing my number into her contact list, I smile. "Don't

worry. I'll wear a designer suit." I stand and she follows, offering me her hand.

"It was really nice meeting you, Quinton Petty Shay."

I wrap her hand in mine, her skin soft and warm. I find myself not wanting to let go, but if I don't walk away, I may do something we'll both really regret tomorrow. "The pleasure was all mine, Kinsley."

She sees herself out and I head back to where the guys are seated, laughing about who knows what and who cares.

"Dude, where's my beer?" Dex asks when I lower my near empty glass to the table.

"Our bromance is over before it started Dexter. I'm giving all my fake love to someone else."

"Fake love? What are you talking about?"

"Does this have anything to do with Kinsley?" Hawken asks. "I saw you talking to her."

"Yeah." I nod, sliding into the booth. "It does. She told her parents she was dating me."

The shocked expressions looking back at me make me laugh. "She was lying, obviously. She just wanted her parents off her back so I offered to fuck with them with her because why the hell not?"

Zeke chuckles. "So, you're going to pretend to be her boyfriend?"

"Yup."

"Oh, fuck. This ought to be good."

OTHER BOOKS BY SUSAN RENEE

All books are available in Kindle Unlimited

The Chicago Red Tails Series

Off Your Game – Colby Nelson

Unfair Game – Milo Landric

Beyond the Game – Dex Foster

Forbidden Game – Hawken Malone

Saving the Game – Quinton Shay

Bonus Game – Zeke Miller

Remember Colby's brother, Elias Nelson? Here's his story! A spinoff of my Bardstown Series of small town interconnected romances!

NO ONE NEEDS TO KNOW: Accidental Pregnancy

(Elias and Whitney's story)

(Bardstown Series Prequel – Previously entitled SEVEN)

I LOVED YOU THEN

The Bardstown Series

I LIKE ME BETTER: Enemies to Lovers

YOU ARE THE REASON: Second Chance

BEAUTIFUL CRAZY: Friends to Lovers

TAKE YOU HOME: Boss's Daughter

ROMANTIC COMEDIES

Smooch: Arya's Story

Smooches: Hannah's Story

Smooched: Kim's Story

Hole Punched

You Don't Know Jack Schmidt
(The Schmidt Load Novella Book 1)

Schmidt Happens
(The Schmidt Load Novella Book 2)

My Schmidt Smells Like Roses
(The Schmidt Load Novella Book 3)

CONTEMPORARY ROMANCE

The Village series

I'm Fine (The Village Duet #1)

Save Me (The Village Duet #2)

*The Village Duet comes with a content warning.

Please be sure to check out this book's Amazon page before
downloading.

Solving Us

(Big City New Adult Romance)

Surprising Us (a Solving Us novella)

ACKNOWLEDGMENTS

This is the spot I would usually thank a bunch of people for helping me through the process of putting this book together and while I could certainly do that, I feel the need to thank YOU, the READER for you continued support and love through each and every book I write.

This book wasn't easy for me. Not because of the subject manner but because it didn't come together in the way I had planned. My alpha readers really wanted to see more of what happens to Dex after the birth of his child and as many pregnancy troped stories go, the books usually end with the birth. So, after having many chapters already written, my alphas told me no. (ok, they didn't actually say "NO", but they did voice their opinions on wanting to see the birth and all that happens after) and even though I initially panicked, I'm SO GLAD THEY DID.

After the book was finished, I didn't feel great about it. There's no third act breakup. There's no huge conflict between characters. There's no big fight and there's no major climax. What the hell was I thinking?!

I literally lost sleep over this. Anxious beyond measure! But you all took my words in stride and have been nothing but kind and complimentary and encouraging about this story and while I sit here staring at my screen in utter bewilderment, my heart is happy and I am more than grateful to have so many readers and cheerleaders in my corner. Sometimes stepping out of your comfort zone is hard. Sometimes it's scary, but with the right circle of friends and peers around you, you can amazing things! Thank you for being my friends.

To my TIKTOK following, SERIOUSLY FUCKING THANK YOU FOR every single message, like, comment and share. It has been an absolute pleasure getting to know so many of you and I can't wait to experience more Booktok craziness because there is so much fun to be had! Some of you come up with the best one-liners to start my books and I am here for it!!

THANK YOU for continuing to talk about my books. It only takes a spark to light a fire and I appreciate every one of you for being that spark for me!

ABOUT THE AUTHOR

Susan Renee wants to live in a world where paint doesn't smell, Hogwarts is open twenty-four/seven, and everything is covered in glitter. An indie romance author, Susan has written about everything from tacos to tow-trucks, loves writing romantic comedies but also enjoys creating an emotional angsty story from time to time. She lives in Ohio with her husband, kids, two dogs and a cat. Susan holds a Bachelor and Master's degree in Sass and Sarcasm and enjoys laughing at memes, speaking in GIFs and spending an entire day jumping down the TikTok rabbit hole. When she's not writing or playing the role of Mom, her favorite activity is doing the Care Bear stare with her closest friends.

facebook.com/authorsusanrenee

x.com/indiesusanrenee

instagram.com/authorsusanrenee

tiktok.com/@authorsusanrenee

amazon.com/author/susanrenee

goodreads.com/susanrenee

bookbub.com/authors/susan-renee

patreon.com/RomanceReadersandWishfulWriters

Made in United States
North Haven, CT
15 June 2024

53684893R00163